A SADISTIC GAME OF KILL AND RUN

The Chicoms struck without mercy. The jungles echoed with screams of fear as the Reds kidnapped, murdered—and disappeared.

Sometimes the Chinese offered terrifying bargains. A wealthy man would be spared—for a gigantic ransom. A sloe-eyed beauty could escape —in exchange for unlimited use of her body. A high official might live—if he agreed to treason.

It was a hell on earth, but about par for the course in strife-torn Indonesia. Except this time something really big lurked behind the blood bath, something that spelled disaster in hideous, nuclear terms—for the entire world!

That's where America—and Nick Carter— came in!

THE NICK CARTER

AX0238	THE DEVIL'S COCKPIT	AS0921	THE SEA TRAP
AX0277	THE BRIGHT BLUE DEATH	AS0923	DOUBLE IDENTITY
AX0288	WEB OF SPIES	AS0928	THE AMAZON
AX0289	SPY CASTLE	AS0938	CARNIVAL FOR KILLING
AX0295	OPERATION MOON ROCKET	AS0940	THE CHINESE PAYMASTER
AX0310	THE TERRIBLE ONES	AS0941	THE DOOMSDAY FORMULA
AX0311	DRAGON FLAME	AN1001	THE CAIRO MAFIA
AX0312	HANOI	AN1016	THE INCA DEATH SQUAD
AX0313	OPERATION STARVATION	AN1033	THE OMEGA TERROR
AX0423	THE RED RAYS	AN1088	ICE BOMB ZERO
AX0424	PEKING/THE TULIP AFFAIR	AN1089	THE RED GUARD
AX0455	BERLIN	AN1090	JEWEL OF DOOM
AX0509	OPERATION CHE GUEVARA	AN1091	MOSCOW
AX0559	OPERATION SNAKE	AN1093	THE MIND KILLERS
AX0560	THE CASBAH KILLERS	AN1094	THE WEAPON OF NIGHT
AX0583	THE ARAB PLAGUE	AN1095	ISTANBUL
AX0584	THE RED REBELLION	AN1097	RHODESIA
AX0622	RUN, SPY, RUN	AN1098	MARK OF COSA NOSTRA
AX0623	SAFARI FOR SPIES	AN1099	MACAO
AX0625	SAIGON	AN1100	THE 13TH SPY
AX0628	AMSTERDAM	AN1101	FRAULEIN SPY
AX0632	MISSION TO VENICE	AN1102	THE GOLDEN SERPENT
AX0634	A KOREAN TIGER	AN1103	THE LIVING DEATH
AX0636	THE MIND POISONERS	AN1109	BUTCHER OF BELGRADE
AX0638	THE CHINA DOLL		
AX0639	CHECKMATE IN RIO		
AX0686	CAMBODIA		
AS0703	THE DEATH STRAIN	AN1127	THE LIQUIDATOR

KILLMASTER SERIES

AN1132	EYES OF THE TIGER	AQ1387	HOUR OF THE WOLF
AN1133	THE DEVIL'S DOZEN	AQ1388	THE PEKING DOSSIER
AN1146	THE CODE	AQ1393	SEVEN AGAINST GREECE
AN1160	OUR AGENT IN ROME IS MISSING ...	AQ1400	THE JERUSALEM FILE
AN1166	THE SPANISH CONNECTION	AQ1401	THE BLACK DEATH
AN1177	DANGER KEY	AQ1414	TARGET DOOMSDAY ISLAND
AN1178	THE DEATH'S HEAD CONSPIRACY	AQ1415	THE FILTHY FIVE
AN1218	ASSIGNMENT: ISRAEL	AY1424	DR. DEATH
AN1227	ICE TRAP TERROR	AQ1439	COUNTERFEIT AGENT
AN1228	HOOD OF DEATH	AQ1440	TEMPLE OF FEAR
AN1244	THE COBRA KILL	AQ1448	14 SECONDS TO HELL
AN1263	VATICAN VENDETTA	AQ1449	SIX BLOODY SUMMER DAYS
AN1264	THE DEFECTOR	AQ1454	ASSASSIN: CODE NAME VULTURE
AN1270	SIGN OF THE COBRA		
AN1271	A BULLET FOR FIDEL	AQ1455	MASSACRE IN MILAN
AQ1297	THE MAN WHO SOLD DEATH	AQ1456	ASSASSINATION BRIGADE
AQ1298	STRIKE FORCE TERROR	AQ1477	AGENT COUNTER-AGENT
AQ1329	CODE NAME: WEREWOLF	AQ1460	THE Z DOCUMENT
AQ1331	NIGHT OF THE AVENGER	AQ1474	THE HUMAN TIME BOMB
AQ1332	THE N3 CONSPIRACY	AQ1479	THE KATMANDU CONTRACT
AQ1333	THE BEIRUT INCIDENT	AQ1486	THE ULTIMATE CODE
AQ1354	DEATH OF THE FALCON	AQ1490	ASSAULT ON ENGLAND
AQ1356	THE AZTEC AVENGER	AQ1493	THE EXECUTIONERS
AQ1370	TIME CLOCK OF DEATH	AQ1501	THE JUDAS SPY
		AQ1502	THE KREMLIN FILE

*Dedicated to The Men of the
Secret Services of the
United States of America*

NICK CARTER

A Killmaster Spy Chiller

THE JUDAS SPY

PRINTING HISTORY

First Award Printing............April 1968
Second Printing..................June 1969
Third Printing...................March 1970
Fourth Printing.............December 1975

This Edition Copyright © 1975 by Universal-Award House, Inc.
All rights reserved, including the right to
reproduce this book or portions thereof in any form.

Produced by Lyle Kenyon Engel

"Nick Carter" is a registered trademark
of The Conde Nast Publications, Inc.
registered in the United States Patent Office.

AWARD BOOKS are published by
Universal-Award House, Inc., a subsidiary of
Universal Publishing and Distributing Corporation
235 East Forty-fifth Street, New York, N.Y. 10017.

Manufactured in the United States of America

Chapter 1

"HOW about their general outline, Akim," Nick said, "can't you recognize *anything?*"

"Just islands. We're so low in the water, it slaps the glass and I can't see clearly."

"How about that sail on the port side?"

Nick was concentrating on dials, his hands busier than an amateur pilot's on his first instrument flight. He squeezed his big frame aside to let the little Indonesian youth twist the periscope mount. Akim sounded weak and scared. "It's a big prau. Sailing away from us."

"I'll take her in further. You watch for something that'll tell you where we are. And for reefs or rocks—"

"It'll be dark in a few minutes and I won't see anything at all," Akim replied. He had the softest voice Nick had ever heard from a man. The pretty little youth was supposed to be eighteen. Man? He sounded as if his voice hadn't changed—or there could be another reason. That would make everything perfect; lost on a hostile shore with a gay first mate.

Nick grinned and felt better. The two-man submarine was a skin diver's plaything, a rich man's toy. It was well made but hard to handle near the surface. Nick held course on 270°, fighting to control buoyancy, pitch, and direction.

Nick said, "Forget the periscope for four minutes. I'm going to let her settle while we close in. At three knots we can't get into much trouble anyway."

"There aren't supposed to be any reefs here," Akim answered. "Fong Island has one, but not on the south. It's a gentle beach. Usually we have good weather. This is one of the last storms of the rainy season, I guess."

In the soft yellow lights of the cramped cockpit Nick peeked at Akim. If the youngster was scared, he was keeping a tight jaw. The smooth planes of his almost pretty face were quiet and composed as ever.

Nick recalled Admiral Richards' confidential comment just before the helicopter took them off the carrier. "I don't know what you're looking for, Mr. Bard, but the place you're going to is a bubbling hell. It looks like paradise but it's pure poison. And watch that little guy. He says he's a Minankabau, but I think he's Javanese."

Nick had been curious. In this business you picked up and remembered every scrap of information. "What could that mean?"

"Beats me. Like a New Yorker claiming he was a dairy farmer from Bellows Falls, Vermont. I spent six months in Djakarta when it was Dutch Batavia. I was interested in the races. One study says there are forty-six types."

After Nick and Akim had boarded the 99,000-ton carrier at Pearl Harbor it had taken Admiral Richards three days to warm up to Nick. The second radio message, delivered on top-secret red paper, had helped. "Mr. Bard" was undoubtedly a nuisance to the Navy, like all State Department or CIA operations, but an admiral led a lonely life.

When Richards discovered that Nick was reserved, pleasant and knew something about ships, he invited the passenger to his spacious cabin—the only one with three portholes on the vessel.

When Richards discovered that Nick knew his old friend, Captain Talbot Hamilton of the Royal Navy, he warmed up to his passenger. Nick rode the elevator from the admiral's cabin up five decks to the flag bridge, watched the catapults hurl Phantom and Skyhawk jets off on a clear-day practice mission, and had a brief look at the computers and complex electronic equipment in the big combat-operations room. He was not invited to try the admiral's white-upholstered revolving chair.

Nick enjoyed Richards' chess and pipe tobacco. The admiral enjoyed testing his passenger's reactions. In fact, Richards had wanted to become a doctor and a psychiatrist, but his father, a shellback Marine colonel, averted that move. "Forget it, Cornelius," he had told the admiral —then a J.G. three years out of Annapolis, "stay with the fleet where promotion begins till you get a crack at a COMCENTER. A Navy doc is a nice spot but a dead end. And you weren't made to hit the outside and have to go to work."

Richards thought that "Al Bard" was a cool customer. An attempt to pump him beyond certain points met with an observation that "Washington has the say on that," and of course you were stopped in the shallows. But Bard was regular—he kept out of the way and respected the Navy. You couldn't ask for much more.

On Nick's last night aboard Richards had said, "I took a quick look at that little sub that came with you. Nicely built but they can be tricky. If you get in trouble right away after the copter puts you in the water, fire a red rocket. I'll ask the pilot to watch for it as long as he can."

"Thank you, sir," Nick replied. "I'll remember that. I checked out the craft for three days in Hawaii. Spent five hours operating it in the sea."

"Was the little guy—what's his name, Akim—with you?"

"Yes."

"Then your weight will be the same. Did you have it in rough sea?

"No."

"Don't take chances—"

Richards had meant well, Nick thought as he tried to run at periscope depth using the horizontal fin-planes. So had the designers of this tub. There was a stronger swell as they closed on the island and he could never quite match buoyancy and sailing depth. They bobbed like a Halloween apple.

"Akim—you ever get seasick?"

"Of course not. I learned to swim when I learned to walk."

"Don't forget how tonight."

"Al, I assure you, I can swim better than you can."

"Don't bet on it," Nick answered. The lad might be right. He had probably been in the water all his life. On the other hand Nick Carter, as N3 of AXE, practiced working-in-the-water, as he called it, every few days of *his* life. He stayed in top condition and practiced a great many physical skills to increase his chances of staying alive. The only professions or arts, Nick believed, that demanded a more rigorous life schedule than his were those of circus athletes.

Fifteen minutes later he ran the small sub right onto a hardpan beach. He tumbled out, secured a hawser to the nose hook, and with a lot of help from the rollers tumbling into surf-mist and with some willing but weak tugs from Akim, he got the vessel part way above the waterline and secured it with two lines to a kedge anchor and a giant, banyan-like tree.

Nick used a flashlight to finish the bowline knot in the hawser around the tree. Then he put out the light and stood erect, feeling the coral sand give to his weight. The tropic night had dropped like a blanket. Stars spattered the purple above. From the shoreline the phosphorescence of the sea flickered and reformed. Above the thud and rumble of the breakers he heard jungle sounds. Bird calls and animal screams that were endless if you listened for them.

"Akim—"

"Yes?" The answer came out of the blackness a few feet away.

"Any idea which way we should go?"

"No. Perhaps I can tell in the morning."

"Morning! I wanted to reach Fong Island tonight."

The soft voice replied, "Tonight—tomorrow night— some night next week. It will still be there. The sun will still rise."

Nick snorted with disgust and clambered onto the sub, dug out two light cotton bush blankets, an axe and a folding saw, a packet of sandwiches and a Thermos of coffee. *Mañana*. Why did some cultures develop such a strong taste for the indefinite future? Relax, was their password. Leave it till tomorrow.

He put the gear up on the beach near the edge of the jungle vegetation, using his flash sparingly. Akim helped as much as he could, stumbling in the blackness, and Nick felt a pang of guilt. One of his own mottoes was *easy does it, you'll last longer*. And certainly, since they had met in Hawaii, Akim had behaved admirably and worked as hard as he could, practicing with the submarine, teaching Nick the Indonesian version of Malay and briefing him on local customs.

Akim Machmur was either very valuable to Nick and AXE—or likely to be the death of the former and of inestimable trouble to the latter and the United States. On his way to school in Canada, the youth had slipped into the FBI office in Honolulu with a hair-raising tale of kidnapping and blackmail in Indonesia. The bureau had advised the CIA and AXE, formal procedure in international matters, and David Hawk, Nick's direct superior and director of AXE, had flown with Nick to Hawaii.

"Indonesia is one of the world's hot spots," Hawk had

explained, handing Nick a briefcase of reference material. "They just had a gigantic blood bath, as you know, and the Chicoms are desperately trying to salvage their political power and regain control. The youngster may be describing a local crime ring. They have some beauties. But with Judas and Heinrich Muller on the loose in a big Chinese junk, I detect a smell. Just their game to kidnap youngsters from wealthy families and demand cash and cooperation with the Chicoms. Of course they'd steal the cash and take Chicom money too. The Chicoms aren't stupid, they know it. But where else can you find two international operators who would murder their own relatives for the right price?"

"Akim is genuine?" Nick had asked.

"Yes. CIA-JAK radioed us a picture. And we flew a faculty member all the way down from McGill just for a quick verification. He's the Machmur boy all right. Like most amateurs, he ran and sounded the alarm before he had enough data. He should have stayed with his family and gathered facts. That, Nicholas, is where you come in—"

After a long talk with the soft-spoken Akim, Hawk made a decision. Nick and Akim would go to the key point of activity, the Machmur enclave on Fong Island. Nick was to retain the role in which he was introduced to Akim and which he would use as a cover in Djakarta; he was "Al Bard," an American art importer.

Akim was told that "Mr. Bard" often worked for something called the American secret services. He seemed properly impressed, or perhaps Nick's rugged, tanned appearance and air of firm but gentle confidence helped.

When Hawk produced the two-man sub and they began intensive practice with it, Nick briefly questioned Hawk's judgment. "We could fly in through normal channels," Nick protested. "You could have the sub delivered to me later."

"Trust me, Nicholas," Hawk countered. "I think you'll

agree with me before this case is much older, or after you've talked with Hans Nordenboss, our man in Djakarta. I know you've seen a lot of intrigue and corruption. In Indonesia it's a way of life. You'll appreciate your subtle approach, and you may need the sub."

"Is it armed?"

"No. You'll have fourteen pounds of explosive and your regular weapons."

Now, standing in the tropic night with the sweet-musty smell of the jungle in his nostrils and the roaring jungle sounds in his ears, Nick wished Hawk had come along. Some heavy animal crashed about nearby and Nick whirled toward the sound. He had his special Luger, Wilhelmina, under his arm, and keen-bladed Hugo would slip into his palm at a touch, but this world felt *big,* as if it could take a lot of firepower.

He said into the blackness, "Akim. Can we try and go along the beach?"

"We can try."

"Which way would be logical to reach Fong Island?"

"I don't know."

Nick made a depression in the sand halfway between the jungle-line and the surf and flopped down. Welcome to Indonesia!

Akim joined him. Nick sniffed the sweet aroma of the boy. He rejected his thoughts. Akim had behaved like a good soldier taking orders from a respected sergeant. What if he used perfume? The kid was always in there trying. It wasn't fair to think—

Nick slept with a cat's alertness. Several times he was awakened by jungle sounds, once by a heavy roller that boomed spray on their blankets. He noted the time—4:19. That would be 1219 hours in Washington, the previous day. He hoped Hawk was enjoying a good lunch...

He awoke blinded by the glare of a brilliant dawn sun and startled by a big black shape standing near him. He rolled in the opposite direction, came up with Wilhelmina aimed. Akim shouted, "Don't shoot."

"I wasn't going to," Nick growled.

The shape was the biggest anthropoid ape Nick had ever seen. It was brownish, with small ears, and after a good look through the sparse, reddish-brown long hair Nick saw that it was a female. Nick straightened cautiously and grinned. "An orangutan. Good morning, Mabel."

Akim nodded. "They are often friendly. She's bringing you presents. Look on the sand there."

A few yards from Nick were three ripe, golden papayas. Nick picked one up. "Thanks, Mabel."

"They are the most human-like of apes," Akim offered. "She likes you."

"I'm glad. I need friends." The big animal hurried into the jungle and reappeared in a moment with a strange, oval red fruit.

"Don't eat that," Akim warned. "They can, but it makes some humans sick."

Nick tossed a delicious looking papaya to Akim as Mabel returned. Akim instinctively caught it. Mabel emitted a horrified screech and leaped at Akim!

Akim whirled and tried to dodge but the orangutan moved like an NFL quarterback with the ball and a clear field. She dropped the red fruit, grabbed the papaya away from Akim, hurled it into the sea and began to tear Akim's clothes off. Shirt and pants were ripped away with a single, powerful rending tear for each. The ape was grabbing for a handful of Akim's shorts when Nick yelled, "Hey!" and ran forward. He cuffed the ape alongside the head with his left hand, holding the Luger ready in his right.

"Get away. Allons. Vamos!—" Nick continued to yell *scram* in six languages and gesture toward the jungle.

Mabel—he thought of her as Mabel and actually felt embarrassed as she stumbled backward, holding out one long arm with the palm up in a pleading gesture. She turned slowly and stumbled away into the tangled undergrowth.

He turned to Akim. "So that's why you always seemed odd. Why did you pose as a boy, sweetie? Who are you?"

Akim was a girl, a small-model, beautifully formed female. She was fumbling with the ripped jeans, naked except for a tight band of white cloth that compressed her breasts. She did not hurry or appear flustered as some girls might—she gravely turned the ruined pants this way and that, shaking her pretty head. She had the matter-of-factness and sensible frankness about her lack of clothing Nick had observed at a Balinese party. Indeed, this compact cutie resembled one of the perfectly formed, doll-like beauties who served the temple operators as attractive artists, entertainers or just delightful companions.

Her skin was the shade of light mocha, and her arms and legs, while slim, were molded with hidden muscle as Paul Gauguin would have painted them. Her hips and thighs were an ample frame for her small, flat belly, and Nick realized why "Akim" always wore longish, loose sport shirts, to conceal those beautifully shaped curves.

He felt a pleasant warmth in his own legs and loins as he watched her—and suddenly caught himself as he perceived that the little brown minx was actually posing for him! She was examining the torn cloth over and over again while giving him ample opportunity to examine *her!* She was not being coquettish, there wasn't the slightest hint of simpering condescension. She was just behaving with gamin-like naturalness, because female intuition told her it was an absolutely perfect time to take it easy and impress a handsome man.

"I'm surprised," he said. "I can see you're a lot prettier as a girl than as a boy."

She tilted her head and peeked sideways at him, a mischievous sparkle adding luster to the bright black eyes. As Akim she had, he decided, tried to hold her jaw muscles firmly. Now she looked more than ever like the prettiest of the Balinese dancers or the startlingly lovely Eurasians you saw in Singapore and Hong Kong. Her lips were small and full with just a trace of a pout when composed, and her cheeks were firm, high ovals that you knew would feel wonderfully pliant when you kissed them, like warm marshmallows with muscles. She lowered her dark lashes. "Are you very angry?"

"Oh, no." He holstered the Luger. "You spin a yarn and I wind up lost on a jungle shore and you've cost my country maybe sixty or eighty thousand dollars already." He handed her her shirt, a hopeless rag. "Why should I be angry?"

"I am Tala Machmur," she said. "Akim's sister."

Nick nodded without expression. Probably another lie. A confidential report from Nordenboss had said that Tala Machmur had been among the youngsters grabbed by the kidnappers. "Go on."

"I knew you wouldn't listen to a girl. Nobody does. So I took Akim's papers and pretended to be him to get you to come and help us."

"Long way around. Why?"

"I—I don't understand your question."

"Your family could have slipped word to an American official in Djakarta or gone up to Singapore or Hong Kong and seen us."

"That's just it. Our families *don't want* help! They just want to be left alone. That's why they pay and keep quiet. They are used to it. Everybody is always paying somebody. We pay the politicians and the army and on every business deal. Our families won't even discuss their problems with each other."

Nick recalled Hawk's words, ". . . intrigue and corruption. In Indonesia it's a way of life." As usual, Hawk forecast things-to-come with computer accuracy.

He kicked at a chunk of pink coral. "So your family doesn't want help. I'm just a big surprise you're bringing home. No wonder you were so willing to slip into Fong Island unannounced."

"Please don't be angry." She was struggling with the jeans and shirt. He decided she wouldn't get anywhere with them without a sewing machine, but the view was marvelous. She caught his solemn glance and came to him, holding the shreds of cloth in front of her. "Help us and you'll help your country at the same time. We've been through a bath of blood. Fong Island escaped, it's true, but in Malang just down the coast two thousand people died. And they are still searching the jungle for Chinese."

"So. I thought you hated the Chinese."

"We don't hate anybody. Some of our Chinese people have been here many generations. But when people do wrong things and everybody gets angry they kill. Old resentments. Jealousies. Religious differences."

"Superstition over reason," Nick murmured. He had seen it in action. He patted one smooth brown arm, noting how delicately she was formed. "Well, we're here. Let's find Fong Island."

She waggled the bundle of cloth. "Would you hand me one of the blankets?"

"Here."

He stubbornly refused to turn away and enjoyed looking at her as she dropped the old clothing and deftly turned herself into the blanket which became a sheath-like sarong. Her gleaming black eyes were impish. "It's more comfortable anyway."

"It looks good on you," he said. She uncoiled the white cloth band that restrained her breasts and the sarong was beautifully filled out. "Yes," he added, "delightful. Now where are we?"

She turned and studied the gentle curve of the bay, bordered on its east rim by twisted mangroves. The shore was a white crescent, the sea sapphire in the clear dawn, except where green and azure breakers tumbled over a pink coral reef. Several sea slugs slumped above the surf line like foot-long caterpillars.

"We may be on Adata Island," she said. "It's uninhabited. The family uses it as sort of a zoo. There are crocodiles, snakes and tigers. If we circle to the north shore we can cross to Fong."

"No wonder Conrad Hilton skipped it," Nick said. "Sit down and give me half an hour. Then we'll move out."

He resecured the anchors and covered the little submarine with driftwood and jungle brush until it looked like a pile of debris on the shore. Tala led the way west along the beach. They rounded several small headlands and she exclaimed, "This is Adata. We're on Creese Beach."

"Creese? Knife?"

"A curved dagger. Serpentine I think is the English word."

"How far to Fong?"

"One pot." She giggled.

"Come again?"

"In Malay, one meal. Or about a half day."

Nick swore soundlessly and strode forward. "Come on."

They reached a gully that cut across the beach from the interior, where the jungle rose in the distance as if there were hills. Tala paused. "It might be shorter to go up the trail beside the stream and out to the north. It is harder going, but it is twice as long to stay on the beach and go to the west end of Adata and come back."

"Lead on."

The trail was horrible, with innumerable deadfalls and barrier vines that resisted Nick's axe like metal. The sun was high and viciously hot when Tala paused at a pool from which the stream ran. "This is the high point. I'm sorry. We're not gaining much time. I didn't realize the trail had not been used for a long time."

Nick grunted as he sliced at a liana with the razor edge of stiletto-like Hugo. To his astonishment it cut through more swiftly than the axe. Good old Stuart! The weapons chief of AXE always claimed that Hugo was a sample of the best steel in the world—he would be tickled to hear this. Nick pressed Hugo back in the arm sheath. "Today—tomorrow. The sun will still rise."

Tala laughed. "Thank you. You remember."

He unwrapped some rations. The chocolate was mud, the biscuits soggy dough. He opened some K-type crackers and cheese and they ate them. A movement back on the trail alerted him and his hand swept out Wilhelmina as he hissed, "Down, Tala."

Up the rugged path came Mabel. She looked black again instead of brown in the jungle shadow. Nick said, "Oh, hell," and threw her the chocolate and biscuit. She took the gifts and nibbled happily, looking like a dowager at tea at the Plaza. When she had finished Nick yelled, "Now scram!"

She went away.

After a couple of miles of downhill work they came to a jungle stream about ten yards wide. Tala said, "Wait."

She went to the edge, deftly made a small packet of her sarong and swam to the other side like a slim brown fish. Nick watched admiringly. She called, "I think it's all right. Come on."

Nick removed his rubber-cleated boat shoes, wrapped them with the axe in his shirt. He had taken five or six powerful strokes when he heard Tala shout and saw a movement upstream from the corner of his eye. A gnarled brown log seemed to move out from the near bank under its own outboard motor. Alligator? No, crocodile! And he knew that the crocs were the worst! His reflexes were swift. Too late to waste time turning—and didn't they say splashing helped! He gripped shirt and shoes in one hand, letting the axe go, and plowed ahead with powerful overhand strokes and a wide, crashing flutter kick.

It would be neck and neck! Or would you say jaws and leg? Tala loomed over him. She raised a limb and brought it down—it hit him on the back. The jungle was ripped by an ear-shattering scream and he heard a giant splash behind him. His fingers touched earth and he dropped the packet and dragged himself up on the bank like a seal shoaling on an ice floe. He turned to see Mabel, waist deep in the dark stream, flailing at the crocodile with a giant tree limb.

Tala hurled another branch at the reptile. Nick rubbed his back.

"Ouch," he said. "Her aim is better than yours."

Tala crumpled beside him, sobbing, as if her small body had at last taken too much and the floodgates burst. "Oh, Al, I'm sorry. I'm sorry. I didn't see it. It nearly got you. And you're a good man—you're a good man."

She was stroking his head. Nick looked up and smiled. Mabel withdrew to the other bank and scowled. At least he was sure it was a scowl. "I'm a pretty good man. More."

He held the slim Indonesian girl in his arms for ten minutes until her hysterical gulps subsided. She had not had time to rewrap her sarong and he noted with approval that her plump breasts were beautifully molded, authentic *Playboy* picture material. Didn't they say these people had no shyness about breasts? They only covered them because the civilized ladies insisted. He wanted to touch one. Resisted the impulse and gave a small sigh of self-approval.

When Tala seemed calm, he went to the stream and dragged in his shirt and shoes with a stick. Mabel had vanished.

When they came out onto a beach which was a replica of the one they had left, the sun was at the treeline in the west. Nick said, "One pot, eh? We took a full dinner."

"It was my idea," Tala replied humbly. "We should have gone around."

"I'm teasing you. We probably wouldn't have made any better time. Is that Fong?"

Across a mile of sea, stretching side-to-side as far as one could see and backed by triplet mountains or volcanic cores, was a beach and shoreline. It had a cultivated, civilized look, unlike Adata. Meadows or farmlands rose on the uplands in green and brown oblongs, and there were clusters of what looked like houses. Nick thought he saw a truck or bus on a road as he squinted his keen eyes.

"Any way to signal them? Do you happen to be carrying a mirror?"

"No."

Nick frowned. There had been a complete jungle survival kit in the sub, but it had seemed stupid to lug it all. The matches in his pocket were like mush. He polished Hugo's thin blade and tried to send flashes toward Fong Island, angling the sun's last rays. He figured he might have made some flickers but in this weird country, he thought dourly, who would care?

Tala sat in the sand, her glossy black hair cascading over her shoulders, her small body slumped with weariness. Nick felt the sore tiredness in his own legs and feet and joined her. "I can flash at them all day tomorrow. They'll get the message."

Tala leaned on him. In exhaustion, he thought at first, until a slim hand crept over his forearm and clung. He admired the perfect, moon-shaped creamy circles at the base of her nails. Man, she was a pretty little thing.

She said softly, "You must think I'm horrible. I wanted to do the right thing but it all wound up in a mess."

He squeezed her hand gently. "It just looks worse because you're so tired. Tomorrow I'll explain to your father that you're a heroine. You went for help. There'll be singing and dancing as the whole family celebrates your courage."

She chuckled as if she enjoyed the fantasy. Then gave a big sigh. "You don't know my family. If Akim had done it, maybe. But I'm only a girl."

"Some girl." It was more comfortable with his arm around her. She didn't object. She snuggled.

After awhile his back ached. He slowly lay back on the

sand and she followed like a barnacle. She began to run one small hand lightly over his chest and neck.

The slim fingers stroked his jaw, outlined his lips, patted his eyes. They massaged his forehead and temples with a knowing cleverness that—combined with the day's exercise—almost put him to sleep. Except that when the tantalizing, feathery touch danced over his nipples and belly button he awoke again.

Her lips were soft on his ear. "You are a good man, Al."

"You said that before. You're sure, huh?"

"I know. Mabel knew." She giggled.

"Leave my girl friend out of this," he murmured sleepily.

"Do you have a girl?"

"Sure."

"Is she a beautiful American?"

"No. Unattractive Eskimo, but man she can cook a swell chowder."

"A what?"

"Fish stew."

"I don't really have any boy friend."

"C'mon now. A beautiful little dish like you? Your local lads aren't all blind. And you're smart. Educated. And by the way"—he squeezed a little with the arm around her—"thanks for conking that croc. It took courage."

She gave a pleased gurgle. "It was nothing." The titillating fingers tap-danced just above his belt and Nick sniffed the hot, rich air. *This is how it happens. Warm tropic night—hot blood pounds. Mine is warming, and is pounding such a bad idea?*

He twisted onto his side, clamping Wilhelmina back under his arm. Tala fitted him as snugly as the Luger in the holster.

"No good-looking young man for you over on Fong Island?"

"Not really. Gan Bik Tjang says he loves me, but I think he is confused."

"How confused?"

"He seems nervous around me. He hardly touches me."

"I'm nervous around you. But I love touching—"

"If I had a strong boy friend—or husband—I'd fear nothing."

Nick diverted his hand which had been traveling toward those magnetic young breasts and patted her shoulder. This required thought. A husband? Hah! It would be wise to study the Machmurs before inviting trouble. There were odd customs—like penetrate daughter and we penetrate you. Wouldn't it be nice if they were a tribal type where tradition said it was an honor if you mounted one of their nubile daughters? No such luck.

He dozed. The fingers on his forehead returned, hypnotic at his temples.

Tala's cry awoke him. He started to jump up and a hand pressed down on his chest. The first thing he saw was a shiny knife that looked two-feet long—not far from his nose, with the tip at his throat. It had a symmetrical, serpentine-curved blade. Hands grabbed his arms and legs. He was held by five or six men and they were not weaklings, he decided, after an experimental wrench.

Tala was pulled away from his side.

Nick's eyes followed the gleaming blade up to its holder, a stern-looking young Chinese with very short hair and clean-cut features.

The Chinese asked in excellent English, "Kill him now, Tala?"

"Don't do it till I give you the message," Nick barked. It seemed as smart a thing to say as any.

The Chinese frowned. "I am Gan Bik Tjang. Who are you?"

Chapter 2

"STOP!" Tala shouted.

About time she joined the action, Nick thought. He lay very still and said, "I'm Al Bard, an American businessman. I brought Miss Machmur home."

By rolling his eyes he watched Tala step close to the pig-pile with himself on the bottom. She said, "He is with us, Gan. He brought me back from Hawaii. I talked with the *Orang Americas* and—"

She continued with a stream of Malay-Indonesian which Nick could not follow. Men began to climb off his arms and legs. At last the slim Chinese youth removed the creese and put it carefully in a belt case. He put out an arm and Nick took it as if he needed it. No harm in getting a grip on one of them—just in case. He pretended to be clumsy and appear resentful and frightened, but once on his feet he studied the situation as he stumbled in the sand. Seven men. One holding a repeating shotgun. He would get him first, if need be, and the chances were better than even that he would take them all. Hours and years of practice—judo, karate, savate—and deadly precision with Wilhelmina and Hugo gave you a tremendous edge.

He shook his head and rubbed his arm and staggered closer to the man with the shotgun. "Please excuse us," Gan said. "Tala says you have come to help us. I thought she might be your prisoner. We saw the flash last night and came over before dawn."

"I understand," Nick answered. "No harm done. Glad to meet you. Tala has talked about you."

Gan looked pleased. "Where is your boat?"

Nick shot a warning glance at Tala. "The U.S. Navy dropped us here. On the other side of the island."

"I see. Our boat is just up the beach. Can you make it?"

Nick decided his acting was improving. "I'm fine. How are things at Fong?"

"Not good. Not bad. We have our—troubles."

"Tala told us. Any more word from the bandits?"

"Yes. Always the same. More money or they will kill— the hostages."

Nick was sure he had been going to say "Tala." But Tala was right here! They walked along the beach. Gan said, "You are going to meet Adam Machmur. He will not be happy to see you, you know."

"I've heard. We can offer powerful help. I'm sure Tala told you I also have a government connection. Why won't he and the other victims welcome it?"

"They don't believe in help from governments. They believe in the power of money and their own plans. Their own—I guess the English word is cunning."

"And they don't even cooperate with each other . . ."

"No. It is not the way they think. Each believes that if you pay, everything will come out all right and you can always get more money. You know the story of the goose and the golden eggs?"

"Yes."

"It's like that. They cannot understand how bandits could kill the goose that lays the gold."

"But you think differently—"

They rounded a spit of pink-white sand and Nick saw a small sailing craft, a double-ended outrigger vessel with a large lateen sail half-lowered, flapping in the light breeze. A man was reefing it. He stopped when he saw them. Gan had been silent for several minutes. At last he said, "Some of us are younger. We see and read and think differently."

"Your English is excellent and you have an American rather than a British accent. Did you go to school in the United States?"

"Berkeley," Gan replied shortly.

There was little chance to talk in the prau. The big sail made maximum use of the easy wind and the small craft crossed the patch of sea at four or five knots, with Indonesians draped over its outriggers. They were muscular, hard little men, all bone and sinew, and they were fine sailors. Without a word they would move their weight to maintain the best sailing trim.

In the bright morning Fong Island looked more businesslike than at dusk. They headed for a big dock that stretched out on piles about two hundred yards from the shore. At its landward end was a complex of warehouses and sheds, trucks of several sizes; to the east a small engine was shunting tiny cars in a rail yard.

Nick leaned near Gan's ear. "What do you ship?"

"Rice, kapok, coconut products, coffee, rubber. Tin and bauxite from other islands. Mr. Machmur is very—alert."

"How is business?"

"Mr. Machmur owns a lot of stores. Big one in Djakarta. We never lack for markets except when world prices are way down."

Nick thought that Gan Bik was alert, too. They landed on a floating dock beside the big pier, next to a two-masted schooner into which a mobile crane was loading bags on pallets.

Gan Bik led Tala and Nick along the dock and up a walk with a hard-shell surface to a big, cool-looking building with awning shutters. They entered an office with a picturesque decor in a blend of European and Asian themes; walls of polished wood displayed art that Nick decided was outstanding, two giant fans circled overhead, mocking the tall air-conditioner silent in a corner. The broad ironwood executive desk was flanked by a modern adding machine and a switchboard and recording equipment.

The man at the desk was large—wide, not tall—with keen brown eyes. He wore spotless, tailored white cottons. A dignified Chinese in a linen suit over a light blue polo shirt sat on a bench of rubbed teak. Gan Bik said, "Mr. Machmur—this is Mr. Al Bard. He brought Tala." Nick shook hands and Gan drew him to the Chinese. "This is my father, Ong Tjang."

They were pleasant without changing facial expressions. Nick did not sense hostility—rather an air of "it's nice you've come and it will be nice when you go."

Adam Machmur said, "Tala will want to eat and rest. Gan, please take her to the house in my car and come back."

Tala flashed Nick a glance—*I told you so*—and followed Gan out. The Machmur patriarch gestured Nick to a chair. "Thank you for returning my impetuous daughter. I hope she was no—trouble."

"No trouble at all."

"How did she contact you?"

Nick laid it on the line. He told them what Tala had said in Hawaii and, without identifying AXE, hinted that he was an "agent" of the United States in addition to being an "American art importer." When he stopped talking Adam exchanged looks with Ong Tjang. Nick thought they swapped nods, but reading these two was like trying to guess the hole card of a good five-card stud man.

Adam said, "It is partly true. One of my children has been—er, detained until I meet certain demands. But I would have preferred to keep it in the family. We expect to—reach a solution without any outside help."

"They'll bleed you white," Nick said bluntly.

"We have—considerable resources. And one is never so mad as to kill the golden goose. We want no interference."

"Not interference, Mr. Machmur. Help. Substantial, powerful help if the situation requires it."

"We know your—agents are powerful. I have—met a number of them in the last few years. A Mr. Hans Nordenboss is on his way here by air now. I believe he is an associate of yours. As soon as he arrives I hope you both will enjoy my hospitality for a good meal and then go away."

"You are called a very smart man, Mr. Machmur. Would a smart general reject reinforcements?"

"If they involve additional danger. Mr. Bard—I have over two thousand good men of my own. And I can get as many more quickly if I want them."

"Do they know where the mystery junk is with the prisoners?"

Machmur frowned. "No. But we will in time."

"You've got enough planes of your own to look?"

Ong Tjang coughed politely. "Mr. Bard, it is more complicated than perhaps you know. Our nation is as long as your own continent, but composed of over three thousand islands with an almost infinite number of harbors and hiding places. Thousands of ships come and go. All types. This is the real pirate land. Do you remember any stories? They operate even today. And very efficiently, now, with old sailing ships and new powerful ones that can outrun all but the fastest naval vessels."

Nick nodded. "I've heard that smuggling is still a leading industry. The Philippines protest about it every little while. But now consider Nordenboss. He is an authority on this area. He meets many important people and he listens. And when we get the right lead—we can call on real help. Modern devices that even your thousands of men and many ships can't equal."

"We know," Adam Machmur answered. "However, no matter how much of an—authority Mr. Nordenboss may be this is a different and complex society. I have met Hans Nordenboss. I respect his ability. But I repeat—please leave us alone."

"Will you tell me if there have been new demands?"

The two older men exchanged swift glances again. Nick decided never to play bridge against them. "No. It is not your concern," Machmur said.

"Of course we don't have any authority to conduct an investigation in your country unless you or your authorities want us to," Nick admitted, speaking softly and very politely, as if he had accepted their wishes. "We would like to help, but if we cannot—we cannot. On the other hand, if we should by chance come across something of help to *your* police—I'm sure you would cooperate with us—I mean with them."

Adam Machmur handed Nick a box of short, blunt Dutch cigars. Nick took one, as did Ong Tjang. They puffed for a moment in silence. The cigar was excellent. At last Ong Tjang observed, his face expressionless, "You will find our authorities can be puzzling—from a Western point of view."

"I have heard some comments on their methods," Nick admitted.

"In this area the army is much more important than the police."

"I see."

"They are very poorly paid."

"So they collect a little here and there."

"As uncontrolled armies always have," Ong Tjang agreed suavely. "It is one of the things your Washington and Jefferson and Paine were so aware of and protected your country against."

Nick let his eyes travel swiftly to the Chinaman's face

to see if he was being kidded. Might as well try and read the temperature on a printed calendar. "It must be hard to do business."

"But not impossible," Machmur explained. "Doing business here is like politics, it becomes the art of doing the possible. Only fools want to stop commerce—as long as they get their share."

"So you can handle the authorities. How are you going to cope with the blackmailers and kidnappers when they get rougher?"

"We will discover a way when the time comes. Meanwhile we are careful. Most Indonesian youths from families of importance are now guarded or in school abroad."

"What will you do with Tala?"

"We must discuss it. Perhaps she should go to school in Canada—"

Nick thought he was going to say "also", which would give him an opening to ask about Akim. Instead Adam said swiftly, "Mr. Nordenboss will be here in about two hours. You must be ready for a bath and some food and I'm sure we can outfit you nicely at the store." He stood up. "And I'll give you a little tour of our lands."

His hosts conducted Nick to a parking lot where a Land Rover was being lazily wiped by a young man in a tucked-up outdoor-style sarong. He wore a hibiscus behind one ear, but he drove carefully and well.

They went through a substantial village about a mile from the docks, thronged with people and children, its architecture clearly reflecting a Dutch influence. The inhabitants were colorfully dressed, busy and cheerful, and the area was very clean and neat. "Your town looks prosperous," Nick commented politely.

"Compared to the cities or some of the poor agricultural regions or over-populated ones, we are doing quite well," Adam answered. "Or it may be a matter of how much one needs. We grow so much rice we export it, and we have plenty of livestock. Contrary to what you may have heard, our people are industrious whenever they have something worth doing. If we could get political stability for awhile and put more effort into our birth control programs, I believe we could solve our problems. Indonesia is one of the richest undeveloped areas in the world."

Ong chimed in, "We have been our own worst enemy. But we are learning. Once we cooperate our troubles will be over."

It sounded like whistling in the dark, Nick thought. Kidnappers in the bushes, the army at the door, revolution under foot and half the natives trying to kill the other half because they wouldn't adopt a particular set of superstitions—their troubles weren't nearly over.

They reached another village with a large commercial building at its center, fronting a spacious, grassy square shaded with giant waringin trees. Through the park-like area flowed a small, brownish creek, its banks aflame with bright flowers: poinsettias, hibiscus, azaleas, flame vines and mimosa. The road ran straight through the little settlement, and on either side paths laced intricate patterns to bamboo and thatch houses.

The sign over the store said simply MACHMUR. It was surprisingly well stocked, and Nick was quickly outfitted with new cotton trousers and shirts, rubber-soled shoes and a rakish straw hat. Adam urged him to select more, but Nick refused, explaining that his luggage was in Djakarta. Adam waved aside Nick's suggestion of payment and they went out onto the broad veranda just as two army trucks ground to a halt.

The officer who came up the steps was as hard and straight and brown as a blackthorn cane. You could guess more about his character by the way the few natives lounging in the shade drew back. They didn't seem afraid, just cautious—the way one might retreat from a disease carrier or a dog known to snap. He greeted Adam and Ong in Indonesian-Malay.

Adam said in English, "This is Mr. Al Bard, Colonel Sudirmat—an American buyer." Nick supposed "buyer" gave you a bigger status than "importer." Colonel Sudirmat's handshake was soft, in contrast to his otherwise hard appearance.

The army man said, "Welcome. I had no word you arrived..."

"He came by private helicopter," Adam said quickly. "Nordenboss is on his way."

Brittle dark eyes studied Nick thoughtfully. The Colonel had to look up, and Nick surmised that he hated it. "You are an associate of Mr. Nordenboss?"

"In a way. He is going to help me travel around and look at merchandise. You might say we are old friends."

"Your passport..." Sudirmat held out his hand. Nick saw Adam frown worriedly.

"In my luggage," Nick said with a smile. "Must I bring it over to headquarters? I wasn't told—"

"Not necessary," Sudirmat said. "I'll have a glance at it before I go."

"I'm sorry I didn't know the regulations," Nick said.

"Not regulations. My wish."

They got back into the Land Rover and went along the road, followed by the growling trucks. Adam said softly, "We overplayed our hand. You don't have any passport."

"I will the instant Hans Nordenboss arrives. A perfectly valid passport with visa and entry stamps and whatever is needed. Can we stall Sudirmat till then?"

Adam sighed. "He wants money. I might as well pay him now as later. That will keep us busy for an hour. Bing—stop the car." Adam climbed out and called to the truck which halted behind them, "Leo—let's go back to my office and complete our business and then we can join the others at the house."

"Why not?" Sudirmat answered. "Get in."

Nick and Ong went on in the Land Rover. Ong spat over the side. "A leech. And he has a hundred mouths."

They circled a small mountain terraced and blocked with planting fields. Nick caught Ong's eye and indicated the driver. "Can we talk?"

"Bing is loyal."

"Can you give me any more information about the bandits or kidnappers? I understand they may have Chinese connections."

Ong Tjang nodded somberly. "Everybody in Indonesia has Chinese connections, Mr. Bard. I can tell you are a well-read man. Perhaps you already know that we three million Chinese dominate the economics of 106 million Indonesians. The income of the average Indonesian native is five per cent of that of a Chinese Indonesian. You would call us capitalists. The Indonesians attack us by calling us communists. Isn't it a strange picture?"

"Very. You are saying that you do not and would not cooperate with the bandits if they are connected with the Chicoms."

"The situation speaks for itself," Ong replied sadly. "We are caught between the waves and the rocks. My own son has been threatened. He no longer goes to Djakarta without four or five guards."

"Gan Bik?"

"Yes. Although I have other sons in school in England." Ong wiped his face with a handkerchief. "We don't know anything about China. We have been here for four generations, some of us much longer. The Dutch were persecuting us viciously in 1740. We think of ourselves as Indonesians ... yet when blood runs hot a Chinese face in the street can start stones flying."

Nick sensed that Ong Tjang welcomed a chance to discuss anxieties with an *Orang America*. Why was it, until so recently, Chinese and Americans always seemed to get along? Nick said gently, "I know another race that has experienced senseless hate. Man is a young animal. He acts from emotion much of the time rather than from reason, especially in a mob. Now is your chance to *do* something. Help us. Get information or find out how I can reach the bandits and their sailing junk."

Ong's solemn expression became less inscrutable. He looked sad and worried. "I cannot. You don't understand us as well as you think. We take care of our own problems."

"You mean ignore them. Pay off. Hope for the best. It doesn't work. You just leave yourself open for more demands. Or the man animals I mentioned are gathered up by a power-hungry despot or criminal or politician and you're in real trouble. The time to fight is now. Take up the challenge. Attack."

Ong shook his head slightly and would talk no more. They drove up a long, curving drive to a large house in the shape of a U aimed at the road. It fitted into the tropical landscaping as if it grew with the rest of the luxuriant trees and flowers. It had big wooden awnings and wide screened porches and, Nick judged, about thirty rooms.

Ong exchanged a few words with a pretty young girl in a white sarong and then said to Nick, "She will show you your room, Mr. Bard. She speaks little English, but good Malay and Dutch if you know them. Let us meet in about an hour. In the main room—you can't miss it."

Nick followed the white sarong, admiring its undulations. His room was spacious and had a modern bath in the British style of twenty years ago, complete with a metal rack of towels the size of small blankets. He showered, shaved and brushed his teeth with the equipment ranked neatly in the medicine cabinet, and felt better. He stripped and cleaned Wilhelmina, tightened the harness. To keep a large gun concealed in a sport shirt you needed it perfectly hung.

He lay down on the big bed, admiring the carved wood frame which held the voluminous mosquito netting. The pillows were hard and as long as filled barracks bags; he remembered they were called "Dutch wives." He composed himself and assumed a completely relaxed position, his hands at his sides with palms down, his every muscle softening and gathering refreshed blood and energy as he mentally commanded each minute area of his powerful body to stretch and revitalize itself. It was a Yoga routine he had learned in India, valuable for quickly refreshing oneself, for gathering strength in periods of physical or mental tension, for holding one's breath longer and stimulating clear thinking. He had found some aspects of Yoga to be nonsense, and others invaluable, which wasn't surprising—he had drawn the same conclusions after studying Zen, Christian Science and hypnotism.

He projected his thoughts for a moment to his apartment in Washington, to his small hunting lodge in the Catskills and to David Hawk. The images pleased him. He was feeling alert and self-confident when the door of the room opened—very quietly.

Nick had lain down in his shorts, with the Luger and his knife under his new, neatly folded trousers which lay beside him. He soundlessly put one hand on the gun and tilted his head enough to see the door. Gan Bik came in. His hands were empty. He came toward the bed on feet that made no noise at all.

The young Chinese stopped ten feet away, a slim shape in the gloom of the big, quiet room. "Mr. Bard . . ."

"Yes," Nick answered instantly.

"Mr. Nordenboss will be here in twenty minutes. I thought you would like to know."

"How do you know?"

"A friend of mine on the coast to the west has a radio. He saw the plane and gave me the ETA."

"And you heard about Colonel Sudirmat asking to see my passport and Mr. Machmur or your father asked you to check on Nordenboss and advise me. I can't say much for your fighting spirit around here, but your communications are damn good."

Nick swung his legs over the side of the bed and stood up. He knew that Gan Bik was studying him, wondering about the scars, noting the finely honed physical condition and gauging the strength of the white man's powerful body. Gan Bik shrugged. "The older men are conservative and perhaps they are right. But there are some of us who think very differently."

"Because you've studied the story of the old man who moved the mountain?"

"No. Because we look at the world with our own wide-open eyes. If Sukarno had some good men to help him things would be better. The Dutch didn't want us to get too smart. We've got to catch up on our own."

Nick grinned. "You've got your own intelligence system, young man. Adam Machmur told you about Sudirmat and the passport. Bing told you about my talk with your dad. And the fellow up the coast announced Nordenboss. How about fighting troops? Do you youngsters have a militia organized or a self-defense corps or an underground?"

"Should I tell you if we have?"

"Perhaps not—yet. Don't trust anybody over thirty."

Gan Bik was confused for an instant. "Why? Oh, that's what the American students say."

"Some of them." Nick put on his clothes swiftly and lied blandly, "But don't worry about me."

"Why?"

"I'm twenty-nine."

Gan Bik watched without expression as Nick adjusted Wilhelmina and Hugo. There was no way to conceal the weapons, but Nick got the impression you could squeeze Gan Bik a long time before he would betray secrets. "Shall I bring Nordenboss to you?" Gan Bik asked.

"You are going to meet him?"

"I can."

"Ask him to put my luggage in my room and slip me my passport as soon as he can."

"Will do," the Chinese youth replied and left. Nick gave him time to get down the long corridor and then stepped out into the dark, cool passageway himself. In this wing it had doors on both sides, jalousie-vented doors of natural wood to give the rooms maximum ventilation. Nick chose a door almost across the hall. Neatly placed belongings showed that it was occupied. He closed the door quickly and tried another. The third room he explored was evidently an unused guest chamber. He went in, placed a chair so that he could peek through the door slats and waited.

First to tap on his door was the lad who had worn a flower behind his ear and driven the Land Rover—Bing. Nick waited until the slim youth started down the hall, then stepped silently up behind him and said, "Looking for me?"

The boy jumped, turned, looked embarrassed, then put a note in Nick's hand and hurried away, although Nick said, "Hey, wait—"

The note read, *Look out for Sudirmat. Will see you tonight. T.*

Nick went back to his post behind the door, lit a cigarette for a half-dozen puffs and used the match to burn the missive. A girl's handwriting, and "T." That would be Tala. She didn't know he weighed up men like Sudirmat five seconds after meeting them and then, if possible, told them nothing and never let them get behind him.

It was like watching an interesting play. The pretty girl who had shown him to the room padded softly up, tapped the door of the room, then slipped into it. She carried some linen. It might be needed, or it might be an excuse. She came out in a minute and went away.

Ong Tjang was next. Nick let him tap-tap and depart. There was nothing he wanted to discuss with the elderly

Chinese—yet. Ong would continue his attitude of non-cooperation until events proved it was best to change. The only propaganda wise old Tjang would respect would be example and action.

Next came Colonel Sudirmat, looking like a sneak thief as he pussyfooted along on the matting, watching his back trail like a man who knows he has left enemies behind and some day they will catch up. He tapped. He rapped. He knocked.

Sitting in the darkness, holding one louver of the jalousie open an eighth of an inch, Nick grinned. The fist of authority, ready to open, palm up. He couldn't wait to ask Nick for his passport and he wanted to do it in private in case there was a chance to make a few rupees.

Sudirmat departed, looking displeased. Several people went by, looking bathed and refreshed and dressed for dinner, some in white linen, some in a combination of European and Indonesian fashion. They all looked cool, colorful and comfortable. Adam Machmur went by with a distinguished-looking Indonesian Nick had not met, and Ong Tjang passed with two Chinese of about his own age—well-fed, cautious and prosperous.

At last Hans Nordenboss arrived, carrying a suit-bag, accompanied by a house servant with two pieces of luggage. Nick was across the hall and opening the door of his room before Hans' knuckles hit the panel.

Hans followed him into the room, thanked the youth who departed promptly, and said, "Hi'yuh Nick. Whom I'll call Al from now on. Where did you drop from just then?"

They shook hands and exchanged grins. Nick had worked with Nordenboss once before. He was a short, slightly roly-poly man with close-cropped hair and a merry pudding of a face. The kind who could fool you—the body was muscle and sinew, not fat, and the cheery moonface masked a keen intelligence and a knowledge of

Southeast Asia that was equalled only by a few Britishers and Hollanders who had spent their lives in the region.

Nick said, "I was ducking a Colonel Sudirmat. He wants to see my passport. He came looking for me."

"Gan Bik tipped me." Nordenboss took a leather case from his breast pocket and handed it to Nick. "Here you are, Mr. Bard. In perfect order. You arrived in Djakarta four days ago and stayed with me until yesterday. I brought you some clothes and stuff." He gestured at the cases. "I've got more of your outfit in Djakarta. Including a couple of confidential pieces."

"From Stuart?"

"Yes. He's always eager to have us test his little inventions."

Nick lowered his voice until it barely carried between them. "The kid Akim turned out to be Tala Machmur. Adam and Ong don't want our help. Any line on Judas or Muller or the junk?"

"Just a thread." Hans spoke as softly. "I have a lead in Djakarta that will take you somewhere. The pressure on these rich families is building up, but they're paying off and keeping to themselves."

"Are the Chicoms wiggling back into the political picture?"

"And how. Just in the last few months. They've got money to spend and the Judas ring is putting on political pressure for them, I think. It's weird. Here's Adam Machmur, for instance, a multi-millionaire, giving money to an outfit that wants to wreck him and all like him. And he's damn near forced to smile as he pays."

"But if they haven't got Tala—?"

"Who knows what other member of his family they have? Akim? Or one of his other children?"

"How many does he have?"

"Your guess is as good as mine. Most of these tycoons are Moslems or pretend to be. They have a handful of wives and kids. Hard to check. If you ask him he'll make some reasonable claim—like four. Then you'll find out some day the truth is nearer twelve."

Nick chuckled. "These fascinating native customs." He took a white linen suit out of the suit-bag and swiftly donned it. "That Tala is a cutie. Does he have any more like her?"

"If Adam invites you to a big party, the roast pig bit and dancing the *serempi* and *golek,* you'll see more sweet little dolls than you can count. I attended one here about a year ago. There were a thousand people at the feast for four days."

"Wangle me an invitation."

"You'll get one soon, I imagine, for helping Tala. They are prompt about repaying obligations and fine hosts. We'll fly over for the party when it comes. By the way—you've probably guessed that we won't fly back tonight. Too late. We'll leave first thing in the morning."

Hans led Nick to the giant main room. It had an unobtrusive bar in one corner, a waterfall that refreshed the air, a dance floor and a four-piece combo that played excellent French-style jazz. Nick met a couple of dozen men and women, chatted endlessly, enjoyed a wonderful dinner of *rijsttafel*—a "rice table" with curried lamb and chicken garnished with hardboiled eggs, sliced cucumber, bananas, peanuts, tingling chutney, and fruits and vegetables he could not name. There was thin Indonesian beer and magnificent Danish beer and good whiskies. After the servants withdrew, several couples danced, including Tala and Gan Bik. Colonel Sudirmat drank heavily and ignored Nick.

At eleven forty-six Nick and Hans strolled back along the corridor, agreeing that they had overeaten, enjoyed a wonderful evening and learned not a damned thing.

Nick unpacked, put on a loose cotton robe and made a few notes in his little green notebook in his private code—a shorthand so secretive he once told Hawk, "Nobody can steal it and find out anything. Lots of times I can't figure out what I wrote."

At twelve-twenty there was a tap on the door and he admitted Colonel Sudirmat, flushed with the alcohol he had downed, but still emitting, along with booze fumes, an air of tough power in a small package. The Colonel made a mechanical smile with his thin dark lips. "I didn't want to bother you at dinner. May I see your passport now, Mr. Bard?"

Nick handed him the booklet. Sudirmat inspected it carefully, compared "Mr. Bard" with his photograph, studied the visa pages. "This was issued quite recently, Mr. Bard. You have not been in the importing business very long."

"My old passport expired."

"Oh. Have you been friends with Mr. Nordenboss a long time?"

"Yes."

"I know of his—connections. Do you have them too?"

"I have a lot of connections."

"Ah—that's interesting. Let me know if I can be of help."

Nick gritted his teeth. Sudirmat was looking at the silver cooler which Nick had found on the table in his room, along with a bowl of fruit, tea in a Thermos pot, a dish of cookies and small sandwiches and a box of the fine cigars. Nick waved at the table. "Won't you have a nightcap?"

Sudirmat drank two bottles of beer, ate most of the sandwiches and cookies, and put one of the cigars in his pocket and lit another. Nick parried his half-questions politely. When at last the Colonel stood up Nick was quick to escort him to the door. Sudirmat paused in the opening. "Mr. Bard—we'll have to have another talk if you insist on wearing a gun in my area."

"Gun?" Nick looked down at the thin robe he was wearing.

"The one you had under your shirt this afternoon. I am supposed to enforce all regulations in my area, you know—"

Nick closed the door. It was clear. He could wear his gun, but there would be a personal license fee to Colonel Sudirmat. Nick wondered if the Colonel's troops ever saw their pay. An Indonesian private drew about two dollars a month. He lived by doing in a small way what his officers did on a big scale, grabbing and taking bribes, extorting goods and cash from the citizenry, which accounted for much of the persecution of the Chinese.

Nick's briefing papers on the area had contained some interesting data. He recalled one tip—". . . if involved with the local soldiery, money talks. Most will rent their guns to you or criminals for sixteen dollars a day, no questions asked." He chuckled. Perhaps he would hide Wilhelmina and rent his armament from the Colonel. He put out all the lights except a low wattage lamp and lay down on the big bed.

The tiny, shrill creak that his door hinge made at one point in its turn awoke him instantly. He had practiced listening for it and ordered his senses to monitor it. He watched the panel as it opened, without moving his weight on the high mattress.

Tala Machmur slipped into the room and softly closed the door behind her. "Al—" A soft whisper.

"Right here."

Because the night was warm he had lain down on the top of the bed wearing only a pair of cotton boxer shorts. They had arrived in the luggage Nordenboss brought and were a perfect fit. They should be—they were tailored of the finest available polished cotton, with a hidden pocket in the crotch to hold a *Pierre,* one of the lethal gas pellets which N3 of AXE—Nick Carter alias Al Bard—was authorized to use.

He debated reaching for his robe and decided not to. He and Tala had been through enough together, seen enough of each other, to make at least some convention unnecessary.

She came across the room with short steps, the smile on her small red lips as merry as that of a young girl meeting either a man she admired and was building dreams around, or a man with whom she was already in love. She wore a sarong of very light buff, with flower designs in soft pink and green. Her glossy black hair, which she had worn up at dinner—to Nick's admiring surprise—now cascaded over her smooth brown shoulders.

In the soft amber glow she looked like every man's dream, beautifully curvaceous, moving with a fluid muscle motion that expressed grace propelled by ample strength in the deliciously rounded limbs.

Nick smiled and hitched himself over on the bed, waving an invitation. He whispered, "Hi. Good to see you, Tala. You look absolutely beautiful."

She hesitated for an instant, then carried a hassock over beside the bed and sat with her dark head at his shoulder. "Do you like my family?"

"Very much. And Gan Bik is a nice lad. He has a head on his shoulders."

She made the little shrug and noncommittal blink that girls use to tell a man—especially an older one—that the other or younger man is all right but let's not waste time together talking about *him*. "What are you going to do now, Al? I know my father and Ong Tjang refused your help."

"I'm going to Djakarta with Hans in the morning."

"You won't find the junk or Muller there."

He asked instantly, "Where did you learn about Muller?"

She flushed and looked down at her long, slim fingers. "He is supposed to be one of the gang that rob us."

"And kidnap people like you for a pay-off?"

"Yes."

"Please, Tala." He reached out and took one of the delicate hands, holding it as lightly as he might a bird. "Don't hold back information. Help me so that I can help you. Is there another man with Muller known as Judas or Bormann? A badly crippled man with an accent like Muller's."

She betrayed more than she knew, again, by nodding. "I think so. No—I'm sure of it." She was trying to be honest, but Nick thought—how does she know about Judas' accent?

"Tell me what other families they have a grip on."

"I'm not sure of many. No one talks. But the Loponusias, I am sure, and they have the sons of Chen Hsin Liang and Sung Yu-lin. And a daughter of M. A. King."

"The last three are Chinese?"

"Indonesian Chinese. The Kings live in the Muslim area of North Sumatra. They are practically besieged."

"Do you mean that they might be killed any time?"

"Not exactly. They may be all right as long as M. A. pays the army."

"Will his money hold out until things change?"

"He is very rich."

"Sort of like Adam pays Colonel Sudirmat?"

"Yes, except conditions are worse in Sumatra."

"Anything else you want to tell me?" he asked softly, wondering if she would reveal how she learned about Judas, and why she was free when the information he had indicated she should be a prisoner on the junk.

She shook her lovely head slowly, her long lashes lowered. She had both of her hands on his right hand now, and she knew a lot about skin contact, Nick decided, as her smooth, delicate nails flowed over his flesh like the sweep of butterfly wings. They pattered pleasantly on his inner wrist and traced the veins up his naked arm as she pretended to examine his hand. He felt like an important customer in the salon of an especially pretty manicurist.

She turned his hand over and lightly fingered the fine lines at the base of his fingers, then followed them to the palm and minutely outlined every line on his palm. No, he decided, I'm with the loveliest gypsy fortune teller anyone ever saw—what do they call them in the Orient? Her forefinger crisscrossed from his thumb to his little finger, danced back down to his wrist, and a sudden tingling shiver lanced delightfully from the base of his spine to the hairs at the back of his neck.

"In Djakarta," she whispered in a soft, cooing tone, "you might find out something from Mata Nasut. She is famous. You will probably meet her. She is very beautiful ... much more beautiful than I will ever be. Do not forget me for her." The small black-crested head bent down and he felt her soft, warm lips on his palm. The tip of her small tongue began to circle in its center where her fingers had alerted his every nerve.

The shiver became alternating current. It tingled ecstatically between the crown of his scalp and the tips of his toes. He said, "My dear, you're a girl I'll never forget. The courage you showed in that little sub, the way you kept your head, the blow you aimed at that croc when you saw me in danger—one doesn't forget." He brought his free hand over and stroked the hair of the small head still bent on the palm near his midriff. It felt like heated silk.

Her mouth left his hand and the hassock hitched across the smooth wood floor and her dark eyes came within inches of his. They gleamed like two polished jewels in a temple statue, but they were framed in dark warmth that glowed with life. "You really like me?"

"I think you're one of a kind. You're gorgeous." No lies there, Nick thought, and how far do I go? The little gustings of her sweet breath matched the heightened beat of his own, stimulated by the current she had generated along his spine which now felt like a heated filament encased in his flesh.

"You will help us? And me?"

"I'll do everything I can."

"And you'll come back to see me? Even if Mata Nasut is as beautiful as I say?"

"I promise." His hand, freed, came up behind her cameo-like bare brown shoulders, came to rest above her sarong. It was like the closing of another electric circuit.

The small, pink-tinted lips came within tongue-touch of his own, then softened their plump almost pouty curves in a hoydenish smile that reminded him of the way she had looked in the jungle after Mabel had ripped off her clothes. She dropped her head onto his bare chest and sighed. She made a delightful burden, exuding a warm perfume; a scent he could not type but the aroma of woman was exciting. On his left breast her tongue began the oval dance it had practiced on his palm.

Tala Machmur, tasting the clean-salt skin of this big man who was rarely out of her secret thoughts, felt a moment of confusion. She was no stranger to human emotions and behavior in all its complexities and sensual details. She had never known prudery. She had run naked until she was six, peeked at couples making love time and again in the hot tropic nights, watched carefully the erotic posturings and dances at the late-night feasts when children were supposed to be in bed. She had experimented with Gan Bik and Balum Nidah, the handsomest youth on Fong Island, and there was no part of the male body she had not minutely explored and tested its reactions. Partly in modern protest against unenforceable tabus, she and Gan Bik had copulated a few times, and would have done so far more frequently if he had his way.

But with this *Orang America* she felt so different it aroused caution and question. With Gan it had been *nice*. Tonight she resisted briefly a hot, drawing compulsion that dried her throat so that she must swallow frequently. It was like what the gurus called a self-force that you could *not* resist, as when you thirsted for cool water or hungered after a long day and smelled hot, delicious food.

She told herself—I do not question the wrong-right of it, the way the old women advise because they have found no happiness and would deny it to others. As a modern I consider only the wisdom...

The hair on his great chest tickled her cheek and she looked at the brown-pink nipple standing like a tiny island near her eyes. She marked a damp trail to it with her tongue and kissed its tense-stiff tip and felt him quiver. He was, after all, not very different from Gan or Balum in his reactions, but ah—what a difference in the way she felt toward him. In Hawaii he had always been helpful and quiet, although he must often have thought her a stupid and troublesome "boy." In the submarine and on Adata she had felt that, whatever happened, he would look after her. It was the real reason, she told herself, she had not shown the fear she felt. She had felt safe and secure with *him*. At first she had been surprised by the growing warmth in her, a glow that drew its fuel from the very nearness of the big American; his glance fanned the flames, his touch was gasoline on the fire.

Now, pressed close to him, she was almost overcome by the fiery glow that burned through the core of her like a hot, exciting wick. She wanted to hold him, be held by him, carry him away to keep forever so that the delicious flame would never go out. She wanted to touch and stroke and kiss every part of him, making it hers by right of exploration. She put her small arms around him so tightly that he opened his eyes. "My darling—"

Nick looked down. Gauguin, where are you now when here is a subject for your chalk and brush that cries out to be captured and preserved just as she is right now? Perspiration glowed hotly on her smooth brown neck and back. She was rolling her head on his chest in a rhythm that was nervously hypnotic, alternately kissing him and locking her black eyes on his, exciting him outlandishly with the raw passion that flashed and sparkled from them.

A perfect doll, he thought, a beautiful, ready and eager utter doll.

He grasped her by both arms just below her shoulders and brought her up on top of him, half-on, half-off the bed, and thoroughly kissed the plumpish lips. He was surprised by their flexibility and the feeling of moist ampleness that was quite unique. Savoring their softness and her hot breath and the feel of her against his skin he thought how clever of nature—to give these girls lips that are ideal for making love and for an artist to paint. On canvas they are expressive—against yours the are irresistible.

She left the hassock and with a twist of her supple body brought the rest of her onto him. Brother, he thought as he felt his hard flesh against her luscious curves, it will take some U-turn to change direction now! He realized that she had lightly oiled and perfumed her body—no wonder it glowed so richly as her temperature rose. The fragrance still eluded him; a blend with sandalwood and the essence-oil of some tropical flower?

Tala made a wriggling, snuggling motion that blended her onto him like a caterpillar on a branch. He knew that she could feel every bit of him. After long minutes she gently removed her lips from his and whispered, "I adore you."

Nick said, "You can tell how I feel about you, you beautiful Javanese doll." He ran a finger lightly along the rim of her sarong. "This is in the way and you'll wrinkle it."

She dropped her legs slowly to the floor, stood up, and unwrapped her sarong as casually and unaffectedly as she had when bathing in the jungle. Only now the atmosphere was different. He caught his breath. Her twinkling eyes judged him accurately, and her expression changed to that of a mischievous female urchin, the merry look he had noted before, so appealing because there was no mockery in it—she shared delight *with* you.

She put her hands on her perfect brown hips. "You approve?"

Nick swallowed, swung off the bed and went to the door. No one was in the corridor. He closed the jalousie and the solid inner door which had a flat brass bolt of the quality designed for yachts. He flipped the window jalousies into peek-proof slants.

He returned to the bed and picked her up, handling her like a precious toy, holding her high and watching her smile. Her demure calm was more exciting than activity. He took a deep breath—she looked in the soft light like a nude mannequin colored by Gauguin. She cooed something he could not understand and the soft sound and warmth and scent of her dispelled the doll dream. When he laid her gently on the white spread beside the Dutch wife she gurgled happily. The weight of her generous breasts spread them slightly into inviting, plumped cushions. They rose and fell with a faster than normal beat and he realized their love play had aroused her passions in tune with his own, but she had held them within her, masking the boiling eagerness which he saw clearly now. Her small hands suddenly raised. "Come."

He welded himself to her. He felt an instant of resistance and a small grimace crossed her lovely features to be dispelled at once as if she was reassuring him. Her palms locked inside his armpits, pulled at him with astonishing strength, crawled around his back. He felt the delightful warmth of delicious depths and a thousand tingling tendrils gripping him, relaxed, flickered, tickled, stroked at him moistly and gripped again. His spinal nerve cord became an alternating filament receiving warm, tiny, tingling shocks. The vibration at his loins strengthened powerfully and he was lifted for instants by surges that overwhelmed his own.

He forgot time. Long after their explosive ecstasies had flamed and subsided he moved a damp arm, looked at his wristwatch. "God," he whispered, "Two hours. If anyone is looking for you—"

Fingers danced along his jaw, stroked his neck, flowed down his chest and discovered relaxing flesh. They generated a new, sudden thrill like the vibrating fingers of a concert pianist trilling a staccato passage.

"No one is looking for me." She raised her full lips to his again.

Chapter 3

ON his way to the breakfast room, just after dawn, Nick stepped out onto the wide porch. The sun was a yellow ball in a cloudless sky at the rim of the sea and shore to the east. The landscape beamed fresh and spotless, the road and luxuriant vegetation sloping down to the coastline looked like a minutely crafted model, so lovely it almost lacked reality.

The air was spice scented, still fresh from the night breeze. It could be paradise, he thought, if you banished the Colonel Sudirmats.

Hans Nordenboss came out beside him, his stocky body moving soundlessly on the polished wood deck. "Magnificent, eh?"

"Yes. What's that spice smell?"

"From the groves. Once this area was a mass of spice parks, as they are called. Plantations of everything from nutmeg to peppers. It's a small part of the business now."

"Grand place to live. Too bad men can't just relax and enjoy it."

Three trucks crowded with natives crawled like toys along the road far below. Nordenboss said, "There's part of your problem. Overpopulation. As long as men breed like bugs they'll build their own problems."

Nick nodded. Hans the realist. "I know you're right. I've seen the population tables."

"Did you see Colonel Sudirmat last night?"

"I'm betting you saw him come to my room."

"You win. In fact I listened for a crash and bang."

"He looked at the passport. Hinted that I'd be paying him if I continued to carry a gun."

"Pay him if you have to. He comes cheap to us. His real income is ground out of his own people, big money from types like the Machmurs and pennies from every peasant right down the line. The army is grabbing power again. You'll see the generals in big houses and imported Mercedes-Benz cars. Their base pay is about 2000 rupees a month. That's twelve dollars."

"What a setup for Judas. Do you know a woman called Mata Nasut?"

Nordenboss looked astonished. "Man, you get around. She's the contact I want to put you on. She's the highest paid model in Djakarta, a prime dish. Poses for real stuff and advertising, no tourist junk-art."

Nick felt the invisible support of Hawk's shrewd logic. How appropriate for an art buyer to move in artists' circles. "Tala mentioned her. Whose side is Mata on?"

"Her own, like most everyone you'll meet. She comes from one of the oldest families so she moves in the best circles, yet she gets around among the art crowd and the intelligentsia too. Smart. Takes in a lot of money. Lives high."

"She's not with us or against us—but she knows things we need to know," Nick summed up reflectively. "And she's shrewd. Let's approach her very logically, Hans. Maybe it's best if you don't give me the intro. Let me see if I can find a back stair."

"Go to it." Nordenboss chuckled. "If I were a Greek

god like you instead of a fat old man I'd love to do the exploring."

"Save that fat old man pitch. I've seen you work."

They shared a moment of good-natured banter, the small relaxation of men who live on the edge of precipices, then went into the house for breakfast.

True to Nordenboss' prediction, Adam Machmur invited them to a party two weekends later. After a glance at Hans, Nick accepted.

They drove along the shore to a cove where the Machmurs had a landing ramp for seaplanes and flying boats, facing the sea with a straight run without reefs. On the ramp sat an Ishikawajima-Harima PX-S2 flying boat. Nick stared, recalling recent memorandums from AXE which detailed developments and products. The ship had four GE T64-10 turboprop engines, 110-foot wingspread and a bare-weight of 23 tons.

Nick watched Hans return the wave of a Japanese in a tan uniform without insignia who was releasing tie-downs. "You mean you came down to get me in that?"

"Nothing but the best."

"I expected a four-place job with patches."

"I thought you'd like to ride in style."

Nick computed mentally. "Are you crazy? Hawk will kill us. A four or five thousand dollar charter to pick me up!"

Nordenboss could not keep his face straight. He laughed explosively. "Relax. I wangled it out of the CIA boys. It wasn't doing anything till tomorrow when it's taking some wheels up to Singapore."

Nick gave a sigh of relief that puffed out his cheeks. "That's different. They can stand it—with a budget fifty times ours. Hawk has been keen on expenses lately."

A telephone bell trilled in the little cabin beside the ramp. The Japanese waved at Hans. "For you."

Hans returned frowning. "Company. Colonel Sudirmat and Gan Bik and six soldiers and two of Machmur's men—bodyguards for Gan I suppose—want a lift to Djakarta. I had to say okay."

"Mean anything to us?"

"In this part of the world—anything can mean something. They go to Djakarta all the time. They have some small planes and even a private railroad car. Play it cool and watch."

Their passengers arrived twenty minutes later. The takeoff was unusually smooth, without the usual flying boat's rumble-bump-roar. They followed the coastline and again Nick was reminded of a model landscape as they droned over cultivated fields and plantations, alternating with clumps of jungle forest and oddly smooth meadows. Hans explained the variety below by pointing out that sweeps of volcanic effluvia over the centuries had cleared areas like a natural bulldozer, at times scraping the jungles into the sea.

Djakarta was chaos. Nick and Hans said good-by to the others and at last found a taxi which wove through the teeming streets. Nick was reminded of other Asiatic cities, although Djakarta might be a trifle cleaner and more colorful. The sidewalks were jammed with small brown people, many in gay printed skirts, some in cotton pants and sports shirts, some wearing turbans or big round straw hats—or turbans with big straw hats atop them. Big colored parasols floated along above the crowds. The Chinese seemed to prefer quiet dress in blue or black, Arabian types wore long cloaks and red fezzes. Europeans were quite rare. The majority of the brown people were graceful, relaxed and young.

They passed native markets packed with sheds and stalls. The haggling over every kind of merchandise, live chickens in coops, tubs of live fish and piles of vegetables and fruit was a cackling cacophony of what sounded like a dozen languages. Nordenboss directed the driver—giving Nick a short tour of the capital.

They made a big loop in front of impressive concrete

buildings grouped around an oval green lawn. "Downtown Plaza," Hans explained. "Now we'll see the new buildings and hotels."

They passed some giant structures, several unfinished. Nick said, "It reminds me of a boulevard in Puerto Rico."

"Yes. These were Sukarno's dreams. If he had been less of a dreamer and more of an administrator he might have made it. He carried too much weight from the past. Lacked flexibility."

"I understand he's still popular?"

"That's why he's vegetating. Lives near the weekend palace at Bogor till they finish building him a house. Twenty-five million East Javanese are loyal to him. That's why he's still alive."

"How stable is the new regime?"

Nordenboss snorted. "In a nutshell—they need $550 million annual imports. The export $400 million. The interest and repayments on foreign loans is $530 million. Last I heard there was seven million in the treasury. SNAFU."

Nick studied Nordenboss for a moment. "You talk hard but you sound sorry for them, Hans. I think you like this country and its people."

"Aw, hell, Nick, I do. They've got some wonderful qualities. You'll learn about *gotong-rojong*—helping each to help the other. They are essentially kind except when triggered by their damn superstitions. Wait till you get out into the country. What is called in Latin countries the siesta is *djam karet*. It means the elastic hour. Swim, snooze, talk, make love."

They were leaving the city, passing larger houses along a two-lane road. About five miles out they turned off onto another, narrower road and then into the driveway of a large, wide house of dark wood set amid a small park.

"Yours?" Nick asked.

"All mine."

"What happens when you're transferred?"

"I'm making arrangements," Hans replied rather grimly. "Maybe it won't happen. How many men have we got who speak Indonesian in five flavors as well as Dutch, English and German?"

The house was lovely inside as well as out. Hans gave him a quick tour, explaining how the former *kampong*—wash house and servants' quarters—had been converted to a cabana for the small swimming pool, why he preferred fans to air-conditioning, and showing Nick his collection of shells which filled a room.

They drank beer on the porch, flanked by flame and passion flowers that twisted along the walls in bursts of purple, yellow and orange. Orchids hung in sprays under the eaves, and bright-colored parakeets chattered as their two big cages swung in the light breeze.

Nick finished his beer and said, "Well—I'll freshen up and get into town if you have some transportation."

"Abu will drive you anywhere. He's the lad in the white skirt and black jacket. But take it easy—you just got here."

"Hans, you've gone native." Nick stood up and paced a turn on the broad porch. "Judas is out there with half a dozen captives using them to bleed these people like hogs hung up at slaughter. You say you like them—let's get off our asses and help! To say nothing of our own responsibility to stop Judas pulling a coup for the Chicoms. Why don't you talk to the Loponusias clan?"

"I have," Nordenboss answered quietly. "Have another beer?"

"No."

"Don't sulk."

"I'm going downtown."

"Want me to go with you?"

"No. They must know you by now, don't they?"

"Sure. I'm supposed to be in oil machinery but you can't keep anything quiet around here. Have a late lunch at Mario's. The food is great."

Nick sat on the edge of a chair facing the stocky man. Hans' cherubic features had not lost their merry beam. He said, "Aw, Nick, I'm with you all the way. But around here you use time. You don't buck it. You didn't notice the Machmurs racing around firing blanks, did you? The Loponusias are the same. They'll pay. Wait. Watch. Hope. Maybe they'll get an opening and they'll pounce. These folks are easy-going but they aren't stupid."

"I see your point of view," Nick answered with less heat. "Maybe I'm just a new broom. I want to get connected, learn, spot 'em and go get 'em."

"Thanks for suggesting I'm an old broom."

"You said it, I didn't." Nick gave the older man a gentle slap on the arm. It felt like padded hard leather. "Guess I'm just an eager beaver, eh?"

"No-o. But you're in a new country. You'll learn. I have a native working for me at the Loponusias. If we're lucky we'll know when Judas is about to get paid off again. Then we'll move. We'll know that the junk is somewhere off the north coast of Sumatra."

"If we're lucky. How reliable is your man?"

"Not very. But he'll risk a lot for what I'm paying."

"How about a plane search for the junk? Any use?"

"We've tried. Wait till you fly to some of the other islands and see the amount of shipping around here. It looks like Times Square traffic. Thousands of vessels."

Nick let his big shoulders slump. "I'll nose around town. See you about sixish?"

"I'll be here. Paddling in the pool or playing with my shells." Nick glanced to see if Hans was kidding him. The round countenance was just—merry. His host bounced out of his chair. "C'mon. I'll get you Abu and the car. And for me—another beer."

Abu was a small, slim man with black hair and a strip of white teeth which he flashed frequently. He had removed his jacket and skirt and now wore suntans and a black hat like an overseas cap.

In his pocket Nick had two maps of Djakarta which he had studied carefully. He said, "Abu, please take me to Embassy Row where the art is on sale. You know the spot?"

"Yes. If you want art, Mr. Bard, my cousin has a fine store on Geela Street. Many beautiful things. And on the fences there many artists show their work. He can take you out and make sure you don't get cheated. My cousin is—"

"We'll visit your cousin some day soon," Nick interrupted. "I've got a special reason for going to Embassy Row first. Can you show me where you can park? It doesn't have to be near the art squares. I can walk."

"Sure." Abu turned, the white teeth gleamed, and Nick shivered as they knifed past a truck. "I know."

For two hours Nick looked at art in open-air galleries— some of them just space on barb-wire-topped fences—on the walls in squares, and in more conventional shops. He had studied the subject and was not captivated by the "Bandung School" of hacked out scenes showing volcanoes and rice paddies and bare-breasted women in brilliant blues, purples, oranges, pinks and greens. Some of the statuary was better. "It should be," a dealer told him. "Three hundred sculptors were put out of work when work stopped on Bung Sukarno's National Monument. That's it—up there on Freedom Square."

Rambling along and absorbing impressions Nick reached a large shop with a small title on its window in gold leaf—JOSEF HARIS DALAM, DEALER IN THE FINE. Nick noted reflectively that the goldwork was on the inside of the glass and the folding iron shutters partly concealed at the edges of the windows were as solid as any he had ever seen along New York's Bowery.

The show windows exhibited only a few items, but these were magnificent. In the first were two carved life-size heads, a man and a woman, of some dark wood the color of a well-smoked briar pipe. They blended the realism of photography with the impressionism of art. The man's features expressed calm strength. The woman was beautiful, with a compound of passion and intelligence that caused you to move around the carving to savor the slight changes of expression. The pieces were not colored in any way, all of their grandeur was generated simply by the talent that had worked the rich wood.

In the next window—the shop had four—were three silver bowls. Each was different, each an eye-stopper. Nick made a mental note to keep away from silver. He knew little about it, and he had a hunch that one of the bowls was worth a fortune and the others were common. Unless you knew—it was a refinement of the three-shell game.

The third window held paintings. They were better than those he had been looking at in the open-air stalls and on fences, but produced for the quality tourist trade.

In the fourth window was a portrait of a woman, almost life-size, wearing a simple blue sarong and with a flower over her left ear. The woman looked not quite Asian, although her eyes and skin were brown and the artist had clearly spent a lot of time on her black hair. Nick lit a cigarette and looked—and thought.

She might be a blend of Portuguese and Malay. Her small, pouting lips were like Tala's, but there was a firmness of set that promised passion cautiously given and then beyond imagining. The wide-set eyes above emphatic cheekbones were calmly reserved, yet hinted at daring you unlocked with a secret key.

Nick sighed thoughtfully, stepped on his cigarette and went into the shop. A wiry clerk with a cheery smile became lovingly cordial when Nick gave him one of the cards reading BARD GALLERIES, NEW YORK. ALBERT BARD, VICE PRESIDENT.

Nick said, "I was thinking of buying a few items for

our shops—if we can reach a wholesale arrangement—"
He was led instantly to the rear of the store where the
clerk tapped on a door intricately inlaid with mother of
pearl.

Josef Haris Dalam's large office was a private museum
and treasure room. Dalam read the card, dismissed the
clerk, and shook hands. "Welcome to Dalam's. You have
heard of us?"

"Briefly," Nick lied courteously. "I understand you
have excellent merchandise. Some of the best in Djakarta."

"Some of the best in the world!" Dalam was slim and
short and agile as the village youngsters Nick had seen
climbing trees. His brown face had an actor's ability to
portray instant emotions; as they chatted he looked weary,
alert, calculating, then impish. Nick decided this empathy,
this chameleon flair for matching a visitor's mood, had
brought Dalam from a gutter stand to this substantial
shop. Dalam watched your face and tried on faces the way
you'd try on hats. For Nick the brown features and sparkling
teeth finally settled on a serious-businessman but
cheerful-fellow expression. Nick scowled to see what
would happen and Dalam suddenly looked angry. Nick
laughed and Dalam joined in.

Dalam hopped to a tall case filled with silver work.
"Look. Take your time. Did you ever see the like?"

Nick reached for a bracelet but Dalam was six feet
away. "Here! Gold goes up—yes? Look at this little boat.
Three centuries old. In pennyweight worth a fortune.
Actually priceless. The prices are on the cards."

The priceless price was $4500. Dalam was away, still
talking. "This is *the* place. You will see. Merchandise,
yes, but true art. Irreplaceable, expressive art. Bits of
genius solidified and snatched from the flow of time. And
ideas. Look at this—"

He handed Nick a plump circle of intricately carved
wood the color of rum coke. Nick admired the tiny scene

on each of its sides, the lettering around the rims. He found a silky yellow cord between two sections. "It could be a yo-yo. Hey! It is a yo-yo!"

Dalam matched Nick's smile. "Yes—yes! But what an idea. You know about Tibetan prayer wheels? Spin-spin and stack up prayers in heaven? One of your countrymen made a lot of money selling them rolls of your excellent toilet tissue on which they wrote prayers so that when they spun them they totaled thousands of prayers a spin. Study this yo-yo. Zen, Buddhist, Hindu, and Christian—see, hail Mary full of grace, here! Spin and pray. Play and pray."

Nick studied the carvings more closely. They had been done by an artist who could have inscribed the Bill of Rights on a sword hilt. "Well I'll be—" Under the circumstances he finished with, "—darned."

"Unique?"

"You might say—unbelieveable."

"But you hold it in your hand. People everywhere are uneasy. Worried. Want something to hold onto. Advertise these in New York and see what happens, eh?"

Squinting at the carving Nick saw Arabic, Hebrew, Chinese, Cyrillic lettering that would be prayers. You could study the thing for a long time. Some of the tiny scenes were so finely done a magnifying glass would help.

He dug out the loop of the yellow cord and flipped the yo-yo up and down. "I don't know what would happen. A riot, probably."

"Promote them through the United Nations! All men brothers. Buy your own ecumenical top. And they are nicely balanced, look—"

Dalam performed with another yo-yo. He looped it, walked the dog, spun the whip, and finished with a special trick in which the wooden circle flipped around on half the cord clipped in his teeth.

Nick looked astonished. Dalam dropped the cord and looked astonished. "Never saw the like? Man took a dozen to Tokyo. Sold them. Too conservative to advertise. Still ordered six more."

"How much?"

"Retail twenty dollars."

"Wholesale?"

"How many?"

"Dozen."

"Twelve dollars each."

"Gross."

Nick narrowed his eyes, concentrated on business. Dalam aped him immediately. "Eleven."

"You got a gross?"

"Not quite. Delivery in three days."

"Six dollars apiece. All to be as good as this one. I'll take a gross in three days and another gross as soon as they are ready."

They settled on $7.40. Nick turned the sample over and over in his hand. It was a modest investment to establish "Importer Albert Bard".

Dalam asked softly, his expression thoughtful, matching Nick's, "Payment?"

"Cash. Letter of credit on Bank of Indonesia. You're to handle all the paperwork with customs. Ship by air to my New York gallery, attention Bill Rohde. Okay?"

"Delighted."

"Now I'd like to look at a few paintings..."

Dalam tried to sell him tourist junk of the Bandung school which he kept hidden in an ell of the shop behind drapes. Some he quoted at $125, then dropped to $4.75 "wholesale." Nick just laughed—to be joined by Dalam, who shrugged and went into his next pitch.

When Josef Haris decided that "Albert Bard" could not be had, he showed him some fine work. Nick bought two dozen paintings at an average wholesale price of $17.50 each—and they were really talented work.

They stood before two small oils of a beautiful woman.

She was the woman in the window pictures. Nick said suavely, "She's pretty."

"That is Mata Nasut."

"Indeed." Nick tilted his head doubtfully, as if the brushstrokes displeased him. Dalam confirmed his guess. In this business you rarely revealed what you knew or guessed. He had not told Tala that he had glanced at a half-remembered photo of a Mata Nasut among the sixty-odd Hawk had loaned him . . . he had not told Nordenboss that Josef Haris Dalam had been listed as an important, perhaps politically involved, art dealer . . . he would tell no one that the AXE data sheets listed the Machmurs and Tjangs with a red dot—"questionable—use care."

Dalam said, "The brushwork is unsophisticated. Come out and see what I have in the window."

Nick looked at the painting of Mata Nasut again and she seemed to return his glance mockingly—the reserve as firm in the clear eyes as a velvet barrier rope, the promise of passion boldly shown because the secret key was complete defense.

"She is our leading model," Dalam said. "In New York you remember Lisa Fonseur; we talk of Mata Nasut." He discovered the admiration in Nick's countenance which for a moment was unconcealed. "These are perfect for the New York market, yes? They will stop the walkers on 57th Street, eh? Three hundred and fifty dollars for this one."

"Retail?"

"Oh no. Wholesale."

Nick grinned at the smaller man and received a delighted spread of white teeth in return. "Josef—you're trying to get an edge on me by tripling your prices instead of doubling them. I might go $75 for this portrait. No more. But what I would like is to get four or five more similar to it but posed to my specifications. Can do?"

"Perhaps. I can try."

"I don't need a commission man or a broker. I need an art studio. Forget it."

"Wait!" Dalam's plea was anguished. "Come with me—"

He led the way back through the store, through another heirloom door at the rear, through a twisting passage past storerooms stuffed with merchandise and an office where two small brown men and a woman worked at closely packed desks. Dalam stepped out into a small courtyard with a roof on poles, the adjacent buildings forming its walls.

It was an "art" factory. A dozen painters and wood carvers were industriously and cheerfully at work. Nick strolled through the cramped group, keeping his face carefully expressionless. All the work was good—much of it excellent.

"Art studio," Dalam said. "The best in Djakarta."

"Nice craftsmanship," Nick answered. "Can you arrange for me to meet Mata this evening?"

"Oh, I'm afraid that would be impossible. She is famous, you must understand. She gets plenty of work. She gets fift—twenty-five dollars an hour."

"Okay. Let's go back to your office and finish our business."

Dalam completed a simple order slip and bill of sale. "I will have the customs forms and so forth for you to sign tomorrow. Shall we go over to the bank?"

"Let's."

An officer of the bank took the letter of credit and returned in three minutes with approval. Nick let Dalam see that the account was for $10,000. The art broker was thoughtful as they strolled through the crowded streets on their way back. In front of the shop Nick said, "It's been a pleasure. I'll drop by tomorrow afternoon and sign those papers. Some day we may meet again."

Dalam's response was sheer anguish. "You are unhappy! You don't want the painting of Mata? Here—it is yours at your price." He waved at the lovely face that stared at them from the window—a bit mockingly, Nick thought. "Come in—just for a minute. Have a cool glass of beer—or whisky soda—tea—I beg you to be my guest —as an honor—"

Nick ambled into the shop before tears flowed. He accepted a cold Dutch beer. Dalam beamed. "What else can I do for you? A party? Girls—all the lovely girls you want, all ages, all skills, all kinds? Amateurs, you understand, not professionals. Blue movies? The greatest in color and sound direct from Japan. Watch the movies with the girls—very exciting."

Nick grinned. Dalam grinned.

Nick frowned regretfully. Dalam frowned worriedly.

Nick said, "Sometime soon when I have time I'd love to enjoy your hospitality. You're an interesting man, Dalam my friend, and an artist at heart. A thief by training and background, but an artist at heart. We could do more business. But only if you introduce me to Mata Nasut. Today or tonight. To sweeten your approach you can tell her I'd like to engage her to model for at least ten hours. For that lad you have on the end out there painting heads from photographs. He's good."

"He is my best—"

"I'll pay him well and you'll get your cut. But I'll handle my own deal with Mata." Dalam looked sad. "And if I meet Mata smoothly *and* she poses for your man for my purposes *and* you don't foul up the deal—I promise to buy more of your merchandise for export." Dalam's expressions followed Nick's remarks like a rollercoaster of emotions, but finished on a bright up-cycle.

Dalam exclaimed, "I'll try! For you, Mr. Bard, I'll try anything. You are a man who knows what he wants and is fair with his dealings. Oh, it is good to meet such a man in our—"

"Cut it," Nick said good-naturedly. "Get on the horn and see about Mata."

"Horn?"

"Nickname for telephone."
"Ah yes." Dalam began dialing.

After several calls and much fast talk that Nick couldn't follow, Dalam announced in the triumphal manner of a Caesar proclaiming a victory that Nick might call on Mata Nasut at seven o'clock.

"Very difficult. Very lucky," proclaimed the dealer. "Many people *never* get to meet Mata." Nick had his doubts. The country had had the dollar-shorts a long time. It had been his experience that even the wealthy often move fast for a bundle of cash-on-the-line. Dalam added he had advised Mata that Mr. Albert Bard would pay twenty-five dollars an hour for her services.

"I told you I'd handle my own deal," Nick said. "If she holds me to that it comes out of your side." Dalam looked horrified. "Can I use your phone?"

"Of course. Out of my payment? Is that *fair*? You have no idea what expenses I—"

Nick stopped him talking by putting a hand on his shoulder—like laying a large ham on a child's wrist—and leaning across the desk to look straight into the dark eyes. "You and I are friends now, Josef. Shall we practice *gotong-rojong* and prosper together, or shall we play tricks on each other so we both lose?"

Like a man hypnotized Dalam pushed the phone at Nick without looking down at it. "Yes—oh, yes." The eyes brightened. "Would you like a percentage on future orders? I can mark up the bills and give you—"

"No, my friend. Let us try something new. We'll be honest with my company and with each other."

Dalam seemed disappointed, or troubled by this radical idea. Then he shrugged—the small bones stirring under Nick's hand like a wiry puppy trying to escape—and nodded. "Very well."

Nick patted his shoulder and picked up the phone. He

told Nordenboss he had a late appointment—could he keep Abu and the car?

"Of course," Hans replied. "I'll be here if you need me."

"I'm calling on Mata Nasut to arrange for some pictures."

"Best of luck—lucky. But watch it."

Nick showed Abu the address Dalam had written on a slip of paper and Abu said he knew the way. They passed new houses similar to the cheap projects Nick had seen near San Diego, then an older section where the Dutch influence was again strong. The house was substantial, surrounded by the colorful flowers and vines and lush trees that Nick now associated with the country.

She met him in the airy loggia and gave him a warm firm hand. "I am Mata Nasut. Welcome, Mr. Bard."

Her tones had the clean rich clarity of genuine fancy grade maple syrup, oddly accented, but without a false note. Her name sounded different when she said it; *Nasrsoot*, with the last syllable accented and the double-o pronounced with the soft lurch of *church*, and the long *coo* of *cool*. Later when he tried to imitate her he discovered it took practice, like a real French *tu*.

She had long model's limbs which he thought might be the secret of her success in a land where many women were curved and eye-catching and lovely but built lowslung. She was a thoroughbred among well-rounded Morgans.

They were served highballs in the spacious, airy living room and she said "Yes" to everything. She would pose at home. Dalam's artist would be called as soon as she had time, in two or three days. "Mr. Bard" would be notified to join them and detail his desires.

Everything was settled so easily. Nick gave her his most sincere smile, the guileless one which he refused to admit also gave him a boyish sincerity of expression close to innocence. Mata studied him cooly. "Besides business, Mr. Bard, how do you like our country?"

"I'm surprised by its beauty. We have Florida and California, of course, but they don't compare with the colors, the varieties, of your flowers and trees. And the people—I've never been so charmed."

"But we are so slow . . ." She left it hanging.

"You settled our project faster than I'd have done it in New York."

"Because I know you value time."

He decided the smile on the lovely lips was too long-lasting, and there was certainly a twinkle in the dark eyes. "You're teasing me," he said. "You're going to tell me that your countrymen really make better use of time. They more slowly, gently. More enjoyably, you'll say."

"I might suggest that."

"Well—I think you're right."

His answer surprised her. She had discussed the topic many times with many foreigners. They defended their energy and industry and haste, and they never admitted that *they* might be wrong.

She studied "Mr. Bard," wondering what his angle was. They all had them, the businessmen-CIA operators and the banker-gold-smugglers and the political zealots . . . she had met them all. Bard at least was interesting, the handsomest one she had met in years. He reminded her of someone—a very good actor—Richard Burton? Gregory Peck? She tilted her head to study him and the effect was charming. Nick grinned at her and finished his drink.

Actor, she thought. He is acting, and very well, too. Dalam said he had money—plenty of it.

She decided he was very likeable, for even though he was a giant by local standards, he moved his big graceful body with a gentle humility that made his bulk seem less. So different from some, who swaggered about as if to say, "Move aside, runts." His eyes were so clear and his mouth always pleasantly upcurved. All man, she observed, with that strong man jaw, yet boyish enough not to take things too seriously.

Somewhere in the back of the house a servant clattered a dish and she noted his alertness, the flick of his eyes toward the end of the room. He would be, she concluded with amusement, the most handsome man in Mario's or the Nirwana Supper Club unless sleek dark Toni Poro, the actor, were there. And of course—they were entirely different types.

"You are very beautiful."

Lost in reflection, the soft compliment made her start. She smiled and her even white teeth accented her lips so nicely he wondered how she kissed—he intended to find out. This was some woman. She said, "You are clever, Mr. Bard. That was a wonderful thing to say after the long silence."

"Please call me Al."

"Then you may call me Mata. Have you met a lot of people since you arrived?"

"The Machmurs. Tjangs. A Colonel Sudirmat. Do you know them?"

"Yes. We are a giant country but what you might call the interesting group is small. Perhaps fifty families, but they are usually large."

"And then there is the army . . ."

The dark eyes swept his face. "You learn swiftly, Al. There is the army."

"Tell me something only if you wish—I will never repeat what you say but it might help me. Should I trust Colonel Sudirmat?"

He kept his expression frankly curious, not revealing that he would not trust Colonel Sudirmat to take a suitcase to an airport.

Mata's arched dark brows came together. She leaned forward, her tones very low. "No. Stick to your business and do not ask questions like that of anyone else. The army is in power again. The generals will bank fortunes and the people will explode when they get hungry enough. You are in a web with professional spiders of long practice. Don't become a fly. You are a strong man from a strong country but you can die as swiftly as thousands of others have." She leaned back. "Have you seen much of Djakarta?"

"Just the commercial center and a few of the suburbs. I wish you would show me more of it—say tomorrow afternoon?"

"I will be working."

"Break your appointment. Postpone it."

"Oh, I cannot—"

"If it's money—let me pay you your regular rate—as an escort." He smiled broadly. "A lot more fun than posing in front of hot lights."

"Yes, but—"

"I'll pick you up at noon. Here?"

"Well—" The clatter sounded again from the rear of the house. Mata said, "Excuse me a moment. I hope the cook isn't annoyed."

She went through an arch and Nick waited a few seconds and then swiftly followed. He went through a western style dining room with an oblong table that would seat fourteen or sixteen people. He heard Mata's voice around an L-shaped hallway in which there were three closed doors. He opened the first. A large bedroom. The next was a smaller bedroom, beautifully furnished and evidently Mata's. He opened the next door and jumped through it as a man tried to climb through the window.

"Stop right there," Nick growled. "You won't get ten yards."

Seated on the sill the man froze. Nick saw a white coat and a head of smooth black hair. He said, "C'mon back in. Miss Nasut wants to see you."

The small figure slid slowly to the floor, drew in its leg and turned.

Nick said, "Hello, Gan Bik. Will we call this a coincidence?"

He heard a movement in the door behind him and took his eyes off Gan Bik for an instant. Mata stood in the opening. She held a small blue automatic pointed at him, holding it low and steadily. She said, "I'd call it being where you have no business. What were you looking for, Al?"

Chapter 4

NICK stood still, his mind evaluating his chances like a computer. With an opponent in front and in back—he would take one slug from that peashooter, possibly, before he got them both. He said, "Relax, Mata. I was looking for the bathroom and saw this lad leaving through the window. His name is Gan Bik Tjang."

"I know his name," Mata replied drily. "Do you have weak kidneys, Al?"

"Right now—yes." Nick laughed.

"Put down the gun, Mata," Gan Bik said. "He is an American agent. He brought Tala home and she told him to contact you. I came to tell you and I heard him searching the rooms and he caught me as I was getting out."

"How interesting." Mata lowered the little weapon. Nick noted it as a Baby Nambu. "I think now you both had better go."

Nick said, "I think you're my kind of woman, Mata. How in the world did you get that pistol so fast?"

She had enjoyed his compliments before—Nick hoped this one would soften the chilly atmosphere. Mata led the way into the hall and put the weapon down into a squat vase on a high carved shelf. "I live alone," she said simply.

"Smart." He turned on his friendliest smile. "Can't we all have a drink and talk this over? I think we're all on the same side . . ."

They had the drink, but Nick had no illusions. He was still Al Bard who meant cash money to Mata and Dalam—no matter what his other connections. He drew from Gan Bik the admission that he had come to Mata for the same purpose as Nick—information. With American help at their side, would she tell them what she knew about the next payoff to Judas? Were the Loponusias due to be visited by the junk?

Mata wasn't having any. She said in her calm tones, "Even if I could help you, I'm not sure I would. I do not wish to become involved in politics. I have had a struggle just to survive."

"But Judas holds people who are your friends," Nick said.

"My friends? My dear Al, you do not know who my friends are."

"Do your country a favor then."

"My friends? My country?" She gave a small laugh. "I have been fortunate just to survive. I've learned not to become involved."

Nick gave Gan Bik a lift back to town. The Chinese lad was apologetic. "I wanted to help. I did more harm than good."

"Perhaps not," Nick told him. "You cleared the air with a rush. Mata knows exactly what I want. It's up to me to see if I get it."

With Nordenboss' help, Nick rented a powerboat the next afternoon and took Abu along as pilot. He took his host's waterskis and a hamper of food and drink. They swam, they skied and they talked. Mata dressed was beautiful, Mata in a bikini—which she donned only when they were away from shore—was a vision. Abu swam with them and took a turn on the skis. Nordenboss had said he was absolutely trustworthy because he paid him more than any possible bribe and because he had been with the AXE agent for four years and had made no false moves.

They enjoyed a wonderful day and that evening he took Mata to dinner at the Orientale, then to the night club in the Intercontinental's Hotel Indonesia. She knew a great many people and Nick was kept busy shaking hands and memorizing names.

And she was enjoying herself. He told himself she was happy. They made an impressive couple and she glowed when Josef Dalam joined them for a few moments at the hotel and told her so. Dalam was with a party of six, escorting a lovely girl who, Mata said, was also a much-in-demand model.

"She is pretty," Nick said, "perhaps when she matures she will have your charm."

Djakarta keeps early hours, and shortly before eleven Abu came into the club and caught Nick's eye. Nick nodded, thinking that the man just wanted him to know the car was outside, but Abu came to the table, handed him a note, and left. Nick glanced at it—*Tala here. H.N.*

He handed it to Mata. She read it and said almost mockingly, "So, Al, you have two girls on your hands. She must remember the trip you two had from Hawaii."

"I told you nothing happened, my dear."

"I believe you, yet—"

Their intuition, he thought, as reliable as radar. A good thing she didn't ask him what had happened between him and Tala after they reached the Machmurs—or perhaps she guessed. A short while later, during the drive to her home, she brought up Tala again. "Tala is a charming young lady. She thinks like a foreigner—I mean, she has none of the timidity that we Asian women have developed about some things. She is interested in politics and economics and our country's future. You must enjoy talking with her."

"Oh, I do," Nick said heartily.

"You're teasing me."

"Since you brought up the subject, why not be active in your country's politics? God knows somebody ought to be besides the con men and hustlers and tin soldiers I've seen and read about. The price of rice has tripled in the last six weeks. You see the ragged people trying to buy rice at those wooden barrels the government puts out. I'll bet it is marked up nine times and short-weighted twice before it is served out. I'm a stranger here. I've seen the filthy slums behind the shining Hotel Indonesia, but will you tell me you haven't? Life in your villages may be possible for the poor, in the cities it is hopeless. So let's not make fun of Tala. She's trying to help."

Mata was silent for a long time, then she said without much conviction, "In the rural areas one can get along without money, almost. Our climate—our plentiful agriculture—it's an easy life."

"Is that why you are in the city?"

She came against him and closed her eyes. He felt a tear spatter on the back of his hand. When they stopped at her house she turned to him. "Are you coming in?"

"I hope I'*m* invited. Love to."

"Not hurrying to Tala?"

He led her a few steps from the car and Abu and kissed her gently. "Tell me to—and I'll send Abu back now. I can get a cab in the morning or he can pick me up."

Her weight was tender against him, her hands tight for a moment on his muscles. Then she drew back with a little toss of her magnificent head. "Send him—darling."

When he said he would like to get out of his dinner jacket and cummerbund and tie she led him matter-of-factly to the bedroom with the feminine decor and handed him a hanger. She dropped onto a French rocking-chaise-lounge and looked at him with her exotic face pillowed on her forearms. "Why did you choose to stay with me instead of going to Tala?"

"Why did you invite me?"

"I don't know. Perhaps a feeling of guilt about what you said about me and my country. You meant it. No man would say such things for romantic reasons—they would be too likely to arouse resentment."

He stripped off the maroon cummerbund. "I was being honest, my sweet. Lies have a habit of staying around like spilled tacks. You must be more and more careful and eventually they stick you anyway."

"What did you really think about Gan Bik being here?"

"I haven't decided."

"He is honest, too. You should know that."

"No chance of his being more loyal to his origins?"

"China? He considers himself Indonesian. He has risked a lot to help the Machmurs. And he loves Tala."

Nick sat on the lounge which rocked smoothly, like a giant cradle, and lit two cigarettes. He said softly through blue smoke. "This is a land for love, Mata. Nature made it that and man is trampling all over it. If any of us can help get rid of the Judas types and all the rest who stand on the people's necks, we ought to try. Just because we have our own little comfortable nest and angles we cannot ignore all else. And if we do—someday our pattern will be destroyed in the explosion that is coming."

Tears glistened on the bottom rims of the gorgeous dark eyes. She cried easily—or had a lot of grief stored up. "We are selfish. And I'm like all the rest." She dipped her head onto his chest and he held her.

"It's not your fault. Not anyone's fault. Man has gotten out of hand temporarily. When you spawn like flies and struggle for food like packs of starving dogs with only one small bone for all, there's little time for honesty ... and justice ... and kindness ... and love. But if each of us does what he can—"

"My guru says the same thing, but he believes it is all preordained."

"Does your guru work?"

"Oh, no. He is so holy. It is an honor to give to him."

"How can one talk about justice, if others do the sweating for the food one eats? Is that honest? It seems unkind to the ones who do the sweating."

She gave a little gurgling sob. "You are so practical."

"I don't mean to upset you." He tilted her chin up. "Enough of this serious talk. You made up your own mind whether you want to help us. You're too beautiful to be sad at this time of night." He kissed her, and the cradle-like lounge tilted as he stretched part of his weight along it, carrying her with him. He discovered that her lips were like Tala's, voluptuous and ample, but of the two—ah, he thought, there is no substitute for maturity. He refused to add—experience. She displayed no coyness or false modesty; none of the tricks the amateur thinks aid passion but which only divert it. She stripped him methodically, shedding her own golden gown with one zip, shrug and twist. She studied his dark cream skin against the brown of her own, tested his great arm muscles reflectively, examined his palms as she kissed each of his fingers and made artful patterns of her own hands for his lips to touch.

He found her body in the reality of warm flesh even more stimulating than the promise in the portraits or the soft pressures when they had danced. In soft light the rich cocoa of her skin was delectably flawless except for one dark mole, the size of a nutmeg, on her right buttock. The curves of her hips were pure artistry and her breasts, like Tala's and many of the women he had seen in these fascinating islands, were a visual delight as well as an igniter for the senses when you fondled or kissed them. They were large, perhaps 38C, but so resiliant and perfectly placed and muscle-supported you didn't notice size, you just drew in your breath with a short gulp.

He whispered against the dark, aromatic hair, "It's no wonder you're the most wanted model. You're gorgeous."

"I must reduce." Her matter-of-factness surprised him. "Fortunately for me curved women are favorites here. But when I see Twiggy and some of your New York models, I worry. Styles can change."

Nick chuckled, wondering what kind of a man it would take to trade the soft curves nestled against him for a skinny type you'd have to feel around in a bed to find.

"Why do you laugh?"

"It will go the other way, dear. Comfortable girls with curves are the coming thing."

"Are you sure?"

"Almost. I'll check on it next time I'm in New York or Paris."

"I hope so." She was stroking his hard stomach with the backs of her long fingernails, her head pillowed under his chin. "You are *so* big, Al. And strong. Do you have lots of girls in America?"

"I know a few, but I'm not attached, if that's what you mean."

She kissed his chest, drew patterns on it with her tongue. "Ooh—you still have salt on you. Wait—" She went to her dressing table and brought back a small brown bottle, like a Roman tear urn. "Oil. It's called *Love's Helper*. Isn't that a descriptive name?"

She rubbed him, the slithering stimulus of her palms arousing tantalizing sensations. He amused himself trying Yoga control on his skin, commanding it to ignore the tender hands. It didn't work. So much for Yoga against sex. She massaged him thoroughly, covering every square centimeter of his flesh which began to quiver eagerly at the approach of her fingers. She probed and oiled his ears with delicate artistry, turned him over and he stretched contentedly while butterflies tapped on him from heels to head. When the small flickering fingers flowed around his loins for the second time he discarded control. He removed the bottle which she had propped against him and put it on the floor. He straightened her on the chaise with his powerful arms.

She sighed as his hands and lips flowed over her. "Mmm—that's good."

He brought his face to hers. The dark eyes glowed like twin pools flecked under moonlight. He murmured, "You can *see* what you did to me. Now it's my turn. Can I use up the oil?"

"Yes."

He felt like a sculptor permitted to explore the incomparable lines of a genuine Greek statue with his hands and fingers. This was perfection—this was genuine art—with the exciting difference that Mata Nasut was hotly alive. When he paused to kiss her she made pleased, moaning *hummms* in response to the stimulus of his lips and his hands. When his hands—which, he would be the first to admit, were not inexperienced—caressed erogenous portions of her beautiful body she writhed with pleasure, gave startled gasps of delight while his fingers lingered at sensitive spots.

She put a hand on the back of his head and pulled his lips near hers. "See? *Gotong-rojong.* To share fully—help fully—" She pulled harder and he found himself sinking into an ardent, sultry, peppery-pungent softness where spread lips welcomed his as a torrid tongue lanced suggestively with slow rhythm. Her breathing was faster than her motions, almost fiery with intensity. The hand on his head pulled with surprising power and her other one suddenly hauled at his shoulder—urgently.

He accepted her insistent tugs and settled gently to her guidance, enjoying the sensation of penetrating into a secret, cloying world where time was stopped by rapture. They blended into one pulsating being, inseparable and jubilant, luxuriating in the blissful, sensuous reality which each created for the other. No need for haste, no need to plan or exert effort—the beat, the oscillation, the little twists and spiraling motions came and went, were repeated, varied and modified with unthinking naturalness. His temples were aglow, his stomach and intestines tensed as if he were in an elevator that dropped sharply—and dropped again—and again and again.

Mata gasped once, freeing her lips, and moaned a musical phrase he could not understand before she locked her mouth to his again. Once more his control vanished—who needs it? As she had captured his emotions with her hands on his skin, now she enveloped his whole body and emotions, her burning ardor an irresistible magnet. Her nails closed on his flesh, lightly, like the claws of a playful kitten, and his toes arched in response, a pleasant sympathetic undulation.

"Ahh, now," she murmured, as if from inside his mouth. "Ahh—"

"Yes," he replied, quite willing, "yes, yes—"

For Nick, the next seven days were the most frustrating and fascinating he had ever known. Except for three short photographing appointments, Mata became his full-time guide—and companion. He did not mean to waste the time, but his search for leads and contacts was like dancing in warm cotton candy, and every time he tried to stop someone handed him a cool gin-and-tonic.

Nordenboss approved. "You're learning. Keep moving with that crowd and sooner or later you'll connect with something. If I hear from my plant with the Loponusias we can always fly up there."

Mata and Nick visited the best restaurants and clubs, attended two parties, saw a play and a soccer match. He chartered a plane and they flew to Djokjakarta and Solo, visiting the indescribably wondrous Buddhist sanctuary at Borobudur and the 9th century Prambana Temple. They flew over side-by-side craters containing lakes of different colors, as if you stood above an artist's tray and looked down at his mixtures.

They flew up to Bandung, circling the plateau with its neat rice fields, forests, and cinchona and tea plantations. He was surprised at the unreserved friendliness of the Sundanese, the vivid colors, music, instant laughter. They stayed overnight at the Savoy Homan Hotel and he was astonished at its excellence—or perhaps the presence of Mata cast a rosy glow over his impressions.

For she was marvelous company. She dressed beautifully, behaved impeccably and seemed to know everything and everybody.

Tala was staying in Djakarta, at Nordenboss', and Nick stayed away, wondering what story Tala had used on Adam this time.

But he made good use of her in her absence, on a warm afternoon at a swimming pool in Puntjak. He had taken Mata to the botanical gardens at Bogor in the morning; awed by the hundreds of thousands of varieties of tropical vegetation, they had strolled together like long-term lovers.

After a delicious poolside luncheon he had been silent for a long time until Mata said, "Darling, you're so quiet. What are you thinking about?"

"Tala."

He saw the lustrous dark eyes shed their sleepy closure, widen and glisten. "She's all right, I think, at Hans'."

"She must have gathered a bit of information by now. Anyway I've got to make progress. This idyl has been precious, sweet, but I need help."

"Wait. Time will bring you what you—"

He leaned across to her chaise lounge and stopped the lovely lips with his own. When he drew back he said, "Patience and shuffle the cards, eh? That's all right up to a point. But I cannot let the enemy make all the moves. When we get back to town I must leave you for a few days. You can catch up on your appointments."

The full lips opened, closed. "While you catch up on Tala?"

"I'll see her."

"How nice."

"Perhaps she can help me. Two heads better than one and all that."

On the drive back to Djakarta Mata was silent. As they neared her home, in the rapidly falling dusk, she said, "Let me try."

He enclosed her hand. "Please. Loponusias and the others?"

"Yes. I may be able to learn something."

In the cool, now familiar tropical living room he mixed whiskies-and-sodas, and when she returned from speaking to the servants he said, "Try now."

"Now?"

"There's the telephone. Sweetheart, I'm trusting you. Don't tell me you can't. With your friends and connections—"

As if mesmerized she sat down and picked up the instrument.

He had mixed another drink before she concluded a series of calls, with both languid and swift conversations in Indonesian and Dutch, neither of which he could quite follow. When she replaced the telephone and took the refilled glass, she hung her head for a moment and spoke softly. "In four or five days. At the Loponusias. They are all going there, and it can only mean they all must pay."

"They all? They who?"

"The Loponusias family. It is large. Rich."

"Any politicians or generals in it?"

"No. They are all in business. Big businesses. The generals get money from them."

"Where?"

"At the Loponusias' main property, of course. Sumatra."

"You think Judas must appear?"

I don't know." She looked up and saw his frown. "Yes, yes, what else could it be?"

"Judas holds one of their youngsters?"

"Yes." She swallowed part of her drink.

"What's his name?"

"Amir. He was going to school. He disappeared while in Bombay. They made a big mistake. He was traveling under a different name and they had him stop to do some business and then—he vanished until—"

"Until?"

She spoke so low he could hardly hear. "Until they were asked for money for him."

Nick did not point out that she must have known some of this all along. He said, "Were they asked to do other things?"

"Yes." The swift question caught her. She realized what she had admitted and looked up like a startled fawn.

"Like what?"

"I think—they help the Chinese."

"Not local Chinese—"

"Some."

"But others, too. Perhaps in ships? They have docks?"

"Yes."

Of course, he reflected, how logical! The Java Sea is big but shallow, a trap for subs now that search devices are accurate. But northern Sumatra? Perfect for surface or undersea craft coming down from the South China Sea.

He took her in his arms. "Thanks, darling. When you learn more, tell me. It's not for nothing. I'd have to pay someone for information." He embroidered the half-lie. "You might as well collect, and it's really a patriotic thing to do."

She burst into tears. Ah, women, he mused. Was she crying because he had involved her against her intentions or because he had brought up money? It was too late to retreat. "Three hundred U.S. dollars every two weeks," he said. "They'll let me pay that much for information." He wondered how practical she would become if she knew that he could authorize thirty times that amount in a pinch—more after a talk with Hawk.

The sobs subsided. He kissed her again, sighed and got up. "I've got to go out for a little while."

She looked woeful with tears glistening on the high full cheeks; more beautiful than ever in dismay. He added quickly, "Just business. I'll be back about ten. We'll have a late snack."

Abu drove him to Nordenboss'. Hans and Tala and Gan Bik were seated on cushions around a Japanese cooking stove, Hans jovial in a white apron and tilted chef's hat. He looked like a white-suited Santa Claus. "Hi, Al. Can't stop my cooking. Sit down and get ready for some real food."

A long low table at Hans' left was crowded with dishes; their contents looked and smelled appetizing. The brown girl brought him a large, deep dish. "Not too much for me," Nick said. "I'm not very hungry."

"Wait till you taste it," Hans replied, heaping the dish with brown rice. "I combine the best of Indonesian and Oriental cooking."

The dishes began to circle the table—crab and fish in aromatic sauces, curries, vegetables, spiced fruits. Nick took a small sample of each but the mound of rice was quickly hidden under delicacies.

Tala said, "I've been waiting a long time to talk to you, Al."

"About the Loponusias?"

She looked surprised. "Yes."

"When is it?"

"In four days."

Hans paused with a large silver spoon in the air, then chuckled as he thrust it into red spiced shrimp. "I think Al has a lead on it already."

"I had an idea," Nick said.

Gan Bik looked serious and determined. "What can you do? The Loponusias won't welcome you. I don't even go up there without an invitation. Adam was polite because you brought back Tala, but Siauw Loponusias is—well you'd say in English—a tough one."

"He just won't accept our help, eh?" Nick asked.

"No. Like all the rest, he has determined to go along. Pay and wait."

"And help the Chicoms when he has to, eh? Maybe he really is sympathetic to Peking."

"Oh, no." Gan Bik was emphatic. "He is fabulously wealthy. He has nothing to gain by that. He would lose everything."

"Rich men have cooperated with the Chicoms before."

"Not Siauw," Tala said softly. "I know him well."

Nick looked at Gan Bik. "You want to come with us? It may get rough."

"If it got so rough we killed all the bandits I would be happy. But I cannot." Gan Bik scowled. "I have done what my father sent me here to do—for business—and he has ordered me to return in the morning."

"Can't you make an excuse?"

"You've met my father."

"Yes. I see what you mean."

Tala said, "I'll go with you."

Nick shook his head. "No party for a girl this time."

"You'll need me. With me you may get into the property. Without me you'll be stopped ten miles away."

Nick looked at Hans—surprised and questioning. Hans waited until the maid left. "Tala is right. You'll have to push through a private army in unknown territory. And *rugged* territory."

"A private army?"

Hans nodded. "Not in pretty uniforms. The regulars wouldn't like that. But more efficient than the regulars."

"It's a nice setup. We fight our way through our friends so that we can get at our enemies."

"Change your mind about taking Tala?"

Nick nodded, and Tala's pretty features brightened. "Yes—we'll need all the help we can get."

Three hundred miles north-northwest a strange ship sliced smoothly through the long purple swells of the Java Sea. She had two tall masts, with the big mizzenmast set forward of the rudderpost, and both rigged with topsails. Even an old salt would have to take a second look before saying, "Looks schooner-rigged, but that's a Portagee ketch—see?"

You should forgive the old deepwater man for being half-wrong. The *Oporto* could pass as a Portagee ketch, a handy trader easily maneuverable in tight quarters; given an hour she could be changed into a high-pooped prau, the *Bataka* out of Surabaja; and in another thirty minutes you would blink if you raised your binoculars again and saw a high bow and overhanging stem and odd quadrangular sails. Hail her and you would be told she was the junk *Butterfly Wind* out of Keelung in Taiwan.

You might be told any of these things, depending on how she was disguised—or you might be blown out of the water by a thunder of unexpected firepower from her 40-millimeter gun and two 20mms. Mounted midships, they had 140-degree fields of fire to either side; on her bow and stern recoilless rifles, the new Russian models with handy homemade mounts, filled in the gaps.

In any of her suits of sails she handled well—or she could do eleven knots with her unsuspected Swedish diesels. She was an astonishingly fine Q-ship, built in Port Arthur with Chinese funds for the man called Judas. Her construction had been supervised by Heinrich Muller and naval architect Berthold Geitsch, but it was Judas who conned the financing out of Peking.

A beautiful ship on a peaceful sea—with a devil's disciple as master.

Under a tan canvas awning on the poop deck lounged the man called Judas, enjoying the gentle cottony breeze with Heinrich Muller, Bert Geitsch, and a strange, bitter-faced young man from Mindanao called Nife. If you saw this group and knew something of their individual histories, you would flee, vomit, or grab a weapon and attack them, depending on circumstances and your own background.

Lounging in his deck chair, Judas looked healthy and tanned; he wore a leather and nickel hook device in place of a missing hand, scars laced his limbs, and a vicious wound had left one side of his face askew.

As he fed bits of banana to the pet chimpanzee attached to his chair by a chain, he looked like a genial veteran of half-forgotten wars, a scarred bulldog still good for the pit in a pinch. Those who knew more about him could correct this opinion. Judas was blessed with a brilliant brain and the psyche of a rabid weasel. His monumental ego was a selfishness so pure that to Judas there was only one person in the world—himself. His tenderness to the chimpanzee would last only as long as he felt self-satisfaction. When the animal ceased to please him he would toss it overboard or cut it in two—and explain his actions with warped logic. His attitude with human beings was the same. Even Muller and Geitsch and Nife did not know the real depths of his evil. They survived because they served.

Muller and Geitsch were men stuffed with knowledge and lacking intelligence. They had no imagination beyond their own technical specialties—which were immense—and therefore no regard for others. They could not picture any humanity other than their own.

Nife was a child in a man's body. He killed on command with the empty mind of a baby crowning another with a handy toy to possess a piece of candy. He sat on the deck a few yards forward of the others tossing balanced throwing knives into a foot-square piece of soft wood, hung on a belaying pin twenty feet from him. He threw Spanish overhand, American pioneer undersweep and hand flips from every angle. The blades *kachunged* into the wood with power and precision, and Nife's white teeth flashed each time with a delighted, babyish chortle.

Such a pirate ship, with a demon commanding and fiendish mates, might be crewed by gutter savages, but Judas was far too shrewd for that.

As a recruiter and exploiter of men he had hardly a peer in the world. His fourteen sailors, a mixture of Europeans and Asians and almost all young, were the sweepings from the top of the world's wandering mercenaries. A psychiatrist would have called them insane criminal types, to be locked up for fascinating study. A Mafia *capo* would have treasured them and blessed the day he found them. Judas organized them naval fashion under Geitsch, and like the Caribbean buccaneers, gave them written articles promising fortunes, women and a form of Satanic democracy. Judas would keep the agreement, of course, as long as it served his purpose. The day it did not, he would kill them all as efficiently as possible.

Judas tossed a last piece of banana to the monkey, limped to the rail and pressed a red button. Throughout the ship buzzers sounded—not the harsh clatter of a usual ship's battle gongs, rather the alerting vibrato of a cluster of rattlesnakes. The ship sprang to life.

Geitsch sprang up the ladder to the poop, Muller vanished down a hatch to the engine room. Sailors swept away the awnings, deck chairs, tables and glasses. Wooden falsework along the rails tipped outward and swung down on clattering hinges, a false foredeck house with plastic windows collapsed into a neat square.

The 20mm. guns gave metallic clangs as they were cocked by powerful heaves on their firing handles. The 40mm. clanked behind its canvas screens, which could be dropped in seconds on command.

Judas watched a Peruvian sailor secure ventilators and then speed up a ratline to the foretruck lookout. Men lay hidden behind the poop scuppers above him, showing exactly four inches of their recoilless rifles. The diesels growled as they were started and idled.

Judas checked his watch and waved up to Geitsch. "Very good, Bert. One minute forty-seven seconds I make it."

"Ja." Geitsch had computed it at a minute fifty-two, but you didn't argue with Judas about trifles.

"Pass the word. Three bottles of beer for all hands at lunch. Secure." He reached for the red button and caused the rattlesnakes to buzz four times.

Judas went down a hatch, moving on the ladder with more agility than he did on deck, using his one arm like a monkey. The diesels stopped purring. He met Muller at the ladder to the engine room. "Very good on deck, Hein. Here?"

"Good. Raeder would approve."

Judas suppressed a grin. Muller had donned the brilliant coat and fore-and-aft hat of a British line officer of the 19th century. He removed them now and hung them tenderly in a locker inside his cabin door. Judas said, "They put you into the spirit, eh?"

"Ja. If we had Nelson or they had had a von Moltke or a von Buddenbrock the world would be ours today."

Judas patted his shoulder. "There is still hope. Save that uniform. Come—" They went forward and down one deck. A sailor wearing a sidearm stood up from a stool in the companionway at the forepeak. Judas gestured at a door. The sailor unlocked it with a key from the bunch that swung on a ring. Judas and Muller looked in; Judas flipped the light switch beside the door.

Lying on the bunk was the shape of a girl; her head, covered with a colored scarf, was turned to the wall. Judas said, "Everything all right, Tala?"

"Yes." The reply was short.

"Would you like to join us on deck?"

"No."

Judas chuckled, turned out the light and gestured to the

sailor to lock the door. "She takes her exercise once a day, but that's all. She's never desired our company."

Muller said in a low tone. "Maybe we should drag her out by her hair."

"All in good time," Judas purred. "And here are the boys. I know you'd rather look at them." He paused before a cabin which had no door, just a grill of blue steel. It contained eight bunks, packed against the bulkhead as in older submarines, and five occupants. Four were Indonesians, one a Chinese. They glowered sullenly at Judas and Muller. A slim youth with alert, rebellious eyes who was playing chess stood up and took the two steps to reach the bars.

"When do we get out of this hotbox?"

"The ventilating system is working," Judas replied, his tone emotionless, his words spoken with the slow clarity of one who enjoys demonstrating logic to the less wise. "You are not much warmer than you would be on deck."

"It's damn hot."

"You feel that way because of boredom. Frustration. Be patient, Amir. In a few days we will visit your family. Then we will go back to the island again where you can enjoy the freedom of the compound. This will happen if you are *good* boys. Otherwise—" He shook his head sadly, with the expression of a kindly but strict uncle. "I shall have to turn you over to Heinrich."

"Please don't do that," the youth called Amir said. The other prisoners were suddenly attentive, like schoolboys anticipating a joke on authority. "You know we've been cooperative."

Judas was not fooled, but Muller relished what he thought was respect for power. Judas asked softly, "You are cooperative only because we have the guns. But of course we won't harm you unless it is necessary. You are valuable little pawns. And perhaps before long your families will pay enough so that you'll all go home."

"I hope so," Amir accepted the lie blandly. "But

remember—not Muller. He'll put on his sailor suit and flog one of us and then go into his cabin and—"

"Swine!" Muller roared. He cursed and tried to grab the keys from the guard. His oaths were drowned by howls of laughter from the prisoners. Amir fell on a bunk and rolled with glee. Judas gripped Muller's arm. "Come—they are teasing you."

They reached the deck and Muller muttered, "Brown monkeys. I'd like to strip the hide off all their backs."

"Some day—some day," Judas soothed. "You will probably get all of them to dispose of. After we squeeze all we can out of the game. And I'll have some nice farewell parties with Tala." He licked his lips. They had been at sea five days, and these tropics seemed to keep a man's libido up. He could understand how Muller felt, almost.

"We could start now," Muller suggested. "Tala and one boy wouldn't be missed—"

"No, no, old friend. Patience. The word might get out somehow. The families pay and do what we say for Peking only because they trust us." He started to laugh, a deep-chested sound full of mockery, a parody of humor. Muller giggled, laughed, then began to slap his thigh in time with the ironic cackles that dropped from his thin lips like spilled cutlery.

"They *trust* us. Ah, yes—they trust us!" When they reached the waist where the awning was rigged again, they had to wipe their eyes.

Judas stretched out in his deck chair with a sigh. "We'll stop at Belen tomorrow. Then on to the Loponusias' place. A profitable voyage."

"Two hundred and forty thousand U.S." Muller rolled the figure off his tongue as if it had a delicious taste. "On the sixteenth we rendezvous with the corvette and the submarine. How much must we give them this time?"

"Let us be generous. One full payment. Eighty thousand. If they hear rumors it will fit the amounts."

"Two for us and one for them." Muller chuckled. "Excellent odds."

"For now. When the game is near its end, we'll take all."

"What about the new C.I.A. agent, Bard?"

"He is still interested in us. We must be his assignment. He has gone from the Machmurs to Nordenboss and Mata Nasut. We will meet him personally at the Loponusias village I am sure."

"How nice."

"Yes. And if we can—like the last one—make it look accidental. Logical, you know."

"Of course, old friend. Accidental."

They looked at each other fondly and smiled, like experienced cannibals savoring the memories on their palates.

Chapter 5

HANS Nordenboss was an excellent cook. Nick ate too much, hoping his appetite would return by the time he rejoined Mata. When he was alone with Hans for a few moments in his study he said, "Suppose we leave the morning after tomorrow for the Loponusias—will that give us time to get in, make plans, arrange for action if we don't get cooperation?"

"It's a ten-hour trip the way we have to go. Airstrip is fifty miles from the estates. Roads are fair. And don't plan on any cooperation. Siauw is tough."

"How about your connections there?"

"One man is dead. Another is missing. Maybe they spent the money I paid them too openly, I don't know."

"Let's not tell Gan Bik any more than we have to."

"Of course not, although I think the boy is on the level."

"Is Colonel Sudirmat smart enough to pump him?"

"You mean would the kid sell us out? No. I'd bet against that."

"Do we get any assistance if we need it? Judas or the blackmailers may have their own private army."

Nordenboss shook his head dourly. "The regular army

can be bought for peanuts. Siauw is hostile, we can't use his men."

"Militia? Police?"

"Forget it. Bribery, double-crosses. And tongues that wag for cash paid by anybody."

"Long odds, Hans."

The stocky agent smiled, looking like a genial religionist bestowing a blessing. He held up an ornate shell in his soft-looking, deceptively strong fingers. "But the work is so interesting. Look—intricate—Nature makes trillions of experiments and chuckles at our computers. We little men. Primitive intruders. Aliens on our own ball of mud."

Nick had been through similar dialogs before with Nordenboss. He agreed in patient phrases. "The work is interesting. And the funerals are free if there are any bodies found. Man is a cancer on the planet. You and I have duties ahead. What about weapons?"

"Duty? A precious word to us because we are conditioned." Hans put down the shell with a sigh and displayed another. "Obligation—responsibility. I know your classification, Nicholas. Did you ever read the story of Nero's executioner, Horus? He finally—"

"Can we pack a greasegun in a suitcase?"

"Not advisable. You can hide a couple of handguns or some grenades under a few clothes. Put a few big rupee notes on top, and if our luggage is examined you point to the rupees when the case is opened and chances are the guy looks no further."

"So why not a spraygun the same way?"

"Too big and too valuable. It's a matter of degree. The bribe is worth more than grabbing a man with a handgun, but a man with a machine gun might be worth a lot—or you kill him and rob him and sell the gun as well."

"Charming." Nick sighed. "We'll work with what we can.

Nordenboss gave him a Dutch cigar. "Remember the

latest in tactics—you get your arms from the enemy. He's the cheapest and nearest supply line."

"I've read the book."

"Sometimes in these Asian countries, and especially here, you feel as if you're lost in a crowd of densely packed people. There are no landmarks. You push through them in this direction and that, but it's like being lost in a forest and circling. Suddenly you see the same faces and you know you're wandering aimlessly. You wish you had a compass. You think you're just another face in the crowd, but then you see an expression and a face of terrible hostility. Hate! You wander and another glance catches your eye. Murderous hostility!" Nordenboss put the shell he was holding neatly in its place and closed the case, started for the door to the living room. "It's a new sensation for you. You realize how mistaken you have been—"

"I'm beginning to notice," Nick said. He followed Hans back to the others and said good night.

Before he left the house he slipped into his room and opened a parcel which had been packed in his luggage. It contained six bars of light green soap which gave off a wonderful smell, and three cans of an Aerosol spray shaving cream.

The green cakes were actually plastic explosive. Nick carried igniting caps as standard parts of the pens in his writing case. The fuses were formed by twisting together his special pipe cleaners.

But the cans of "shaving cream" pleased him most. They were another invention of Stuart, the AXE weapons genius. They shot a pink stream for about thirty feet before it broke into a spray that would gag and incapacitate an opponent in five seconds and knock him out in ten. If you could get the spray near his eyes he would be instantly blinded. As far as tests showed, all the effects were temporary. Stuart had said, "The police have a similar device called Klub. I'm naming this AXE."

Nick packed them with a few items of clothing in a dispatch case. Not much against private armies, but when you're about to tangle with the big crowd you take any weapons you've got.

When he told Mata he would be out of town for a few days she knew very well where he was headed. "Don't go," she said. "You won't come back."

"Of course I will," he whispered. They were cuddled on a lounge in the mellow gloom of the patio.

She unbuttoned his sports shirt and her tongue found *the* spot near his heart. He began to tickle her left ear. Since his first introduction to *Love's Helper* they had used up two bottles—perfecting their abilities in achieving, each for the other, greater and more exciting delight. He relaxed as her flickering fingers rippled in the now familiar and always more wonderful rhythms. He said, "You're going to delay me—but only for an hour and a half—"

"Whatever I can have, my darling," she murmured into his chest.

It was the ultimate, he decided—the pulsating beat so adeptly synchronized, the twists and spirals, the sparklers at his temples, the elevator dropping and dropping.

And for her as great a tender impact, he knew, for as she lay soft and replete and panting she hid nothing and the dark eyes glowed wide and misty as she breathed words he barely caught, "Oh, my man—come back—oh, my man—"

As they showered together she said more calmly, "Just because you have money and power behind you, you think nothing can happen to you."

"Not at all. But who would want to harm little me?"

She made a disgusted sound. "The great secret C.I.A. Everybody watches you stumbling around."

"I didn't think it showed so plainly." He hid a grin. "I guess I'm an amateur in a job where they ought to have a professional."

"Not you so much, dear—but the things I've seen and heard about—"

Nick rubbed a giant towel over his face. Let the big company take the credits as long as they collected the lion's share of the brickbats. Or did it prove David Hawk's shrewd efficiency, with his at times annoying insistence on the details of security? Nick often thought that Hawk thrust a man into the posture of an agent—of one of the 27 *other* United States secret services! Nick had once received a medal from the Turkish government engraved to the cover name he had used on that case—*Mr. Horace M. Northcote of the U.S.F.B.I.*

Mata snuggled against him, kissed his cheek. "Stay here. I'll be so lonely."

She smelled delectable, scrubbed and perfumed and powdered. He enfolded her in his arms. "I leave at eight in the morning. You can finish those pictures for me at Josef Dalam's. Send them along to New York. Meanwhile my sweet—"

He picked her up and carried her lightly back to the patio, where he kept her so delightfully busy she had no time to worry.

Nick was pleased by the efficiency with which Nordenboss organized their trip. He had discovered the chaos and fantastic delays which were part of Indonesian affairs, and he expected them. There were none. They flew to a landing strip in Sumatra in an old De Havilland, climbed into a British-made Ford and rolled north through the coastal foothills.

Abu and Tala chatted in a mixture of languages. Nick studied the villages through which they passed, and realized why the State Department paper had said—*fortunately the people can exist without money.* Crops grew everywhere and fruit trees clustered around the houses.

"Some of those little homes look comfortable," Nick observed.

"You wouldn't think so if you lived in one," Nordenboss told him. "It's a different way of life. To keep down the insects you put up with foot-long lizards. Called geckos because they croak *gecko-gecko-gecko*. There are tarantulas bigger than your fist. They look like crabs. Big black beetles can eat toothpaste right through the tube and chew the bindings off books for dessert."

Nick sighed—disillusioned. The terraced rice fields, like giant stairs, and neat villages looked so inviting. The natives seemed clean, except for some with black teeth who spat red betel juice.

The day had become hot. When they drove under tall trees they seemed to pass through green-shadowed cool tunnels, then the open road felt like an inferno. They stopped at a road block where a dozen soldiers lounged under thatched roofs on poles. Abu talked rapidly in a dialect Nick could not follow. Nordenboss climbed out and went into the hut with a short lieutenant, returned at once and they drove on. "A few rupees," he said. "That was the last regular army post. The next we see will be Siauw's men."

"Why the roadblock?"

"To stop bandits. Rioters. Suspicious travelers. It's really nonsense. Anybody that can pay can pass."

They approached a town of larger, sturdier looking buildings. Another inspection point at the near entrance to the town was marked by a colored pole lowered across the road. "Siauw's southernmost village," Nordenboss said. "We're about fifteen miles from his home."

Abu pulled into the turnout. Three men in dull green uniforms came out of the small building. The one with sergeant's stripes recognized Nordenboss. "Hello," he said in Dutch with a big smile. "You stop here."

"Sure we do." Hans climbed out. "C'mon Nick, Tala.

Stretch your legs. Hello, Kris. We've got to see Siauw on important business."

The sergeant's teeth were sparkling white, unstained by betel. "You stop here. Orders. You must go back."

Nick followed his stocky associate into the building. It was cool and dark. Fans turned slowly, powered by ropes that disappeared into the walls. Nordenboss handed the sergeant a small envelope. The man peeked into it, then placed it slowly and regretfully on a desk. "I cannot," he said sadly. "Mr. Loponusias was so definite. Especially about you and any of your friends, Mr. Nordenboss."

Nick heard Nordenboss murmur, "I can make it a little more."

"No. It is so sad."

Hans turned to Nick and said rapidly in English. "He means it."

"Can we fade back and pull a spinner or an end run?"

"If you think you can get through dozens of line backers. I won't bet on gaining any yardage."

Nick frowned. Lost in the crowd without a compass. Tala said, "Let me talk to Siauw. Perhaps I can help."
Nordenboss nodded. "It's as good a try as any. Okay, Mr. Bard?"

"Go ahead."

The sergeant protested that he dared not telephone Siauw—until Hans gestured to him to pick up the envelope. A minute later he held out the phone to Tala. Nordenboss interpreted as she chatted with the unseen Loponusias potentate.

"... she says yes, it is really Tala Machmur. Can't he recognize her voice? She says no, she cannot tell him on the phone. She must see him. It is simple—whatever it is. She wants to see him—with her friends—just for a few minutes—"

Tala talked on, smiled, then held out the instrument to the sergeant. He received some orders and replied with great respect.

Kris, the sergeant, gave some orders to one of his men who climbed into the car with them. Hans said, "Well done, Tala. I didn't know you had a secret that is so persuasive."

She gave him her beautiful smile. "We are old friends."

She revealed no more. Nick had an excellent idea what the secret was.

They drove over the lip of a long, oval valley with its far side next to the sea. A cluster of buildings appeared below and on the coastline there were docks, warehouses and activity among trucks and ships. "Loponusias country," Hans said. "His lands go right up to the mountains. Held in other names, a lot of them. Their agricultural sales are tremendous and they've got a finger in oil and a lot of the new factories."

"And they'd like to keep them. Perhaps that'll give us leverage."

"Don't count on it. They've seen invaders and politicians come and go."

Siauw Loponusias met them amid a bevy of aides and retainers on a screened porch as big as a basketball court. He was a rotund man with an easy smile that you could figure meant nothing. His plump brown face had an odd firmness, his jowls did not sag, his high cheeks looked like six-ounce boxing gloves. He came across the polished floor and embraced Tala briefly and then studied her from several angles. "It is you. I could not believe it. We heard—differently." He looked at Nick and Hans and nodded as Tala introduced Nick. "Welcome. I am sorry you cannot stay long. Let us have something cool to drink."

Nick sat in a large bamboo chair and drank lemonade. The lawns and brilliant landscaping stretched away for 500 yards. In a parking lot there were two Chevrolet trucks, a shiny Cadillac, a pair of Volkswagens that looked brand new, and several assorted British cars and a Soviet-made jeep. A dozen men were either standing guard or patrolling. They were dressed enough alike to be soldiers, and all carried slung rifles or belt holsters. Some had both.

"—give my best wishes to your father," he heard Siauw say. "I plan to see him next month. I will fly directly to Fong."

"But we would like to see your lovely lands," Tala purred. "Mr. Bard is an importer. He had placed large orders in Djakarta."

"Mr. Bard and Mr. Nordenboss are also agents of the United States." Siauw chuckled. "I find out things too, Tala."

She glanced helplessly at Hans and Nick. Nick hitched his chair a few inches toward them. "Mr. Loponusias. We know that the men who hold your son will come here soon in their ship. Let us help you. Take him back. *Now.*"

You couldn't read a thing on the brown bumps with the sharp eyes and the smile, but it took him a long time to answer. That was a good sign. He was thinking.

At last Siauw gave a tiny negative shake of his head. "You find out things too, Mr. Bard. I will not say if you are right or wrong. But we cannot take advantage of your generous help."

"You'll toss meat to the tiger and hope he'll give up his prey and go away. You know tigers better than I. Do you think that will really happen?"

"Meanwhile—we study the animal."

"You listen to his lies. You have been promised that after a few payments and under certain conditions your son will be returned. What guarantee have you?"

"Unless the tiger is insane, it is to his advantage to keep his word."

"Believe me—this tiger is mad. As mad as a man *amok.*"

Siauw blinked. "You know *amok?*"

"Not as well as you. Perhaps you will tell me about it. How a man is crazed into a murderous frenzy. He knows only killing. You cannot reason with him, much less trust him."

Siauw was worried. He had had many experiences with the Malay insanity, *amok*. A wild madness to slay, stab, cut—so powerfully vicious that it helped the U.S. Army decide to adopt the Colt .45 on the theory that the big slug had more stopping power. Nick knew that men in the throes of *amok* had still needed several slugs from the big automatics to stop them. No matter the size of your gun, you still had to put your slugs in the right place.

"This is different," Siauw said at last. "These are— businessmen. We—they—do not run *amok*."

"These men are worse. They are running *amok* now. Into the face of five-inch shells and nuclear bombs. How mad can you get?"

"I—don't quite understand—"

"Can I speak freely?" Nick gestured at the other men grouped near the patriarch.

"Go on—go on. They are all my relatives and friends. Anyway, most of them don't understand English."

"You've been asked to help Peking. They say just a little. Perhaps politically. You might even have been asked to help Indonesian Chinese escape, if their politics are right. You think this gives you some leverage and protection against a man we call Judas. It won't. He steals from the Chicoms as well as you. When the reckoning comes you'll face not only Judas *amok* but the wrath of Big Red Daddy."

Nick thought he saw Siauw's throat muscles move as he swallowed. He imagined the man's thoughts. If there was anything he knew all about, it was bribery and double-triple crosses. He said, "They have too much at stake . . ." But his tone was weaker and the words trailed off.

"You think Big Daddy has controls on these men. It's not so. Judas conned them out of his pirate ship and he has his own men as crew. He is an independent bandit robbing both sides. The instant there is trouble your son and his other captives go over the side with chains on them."

Siauw no longer slouched in his chair. "How do you know all this?"

"You said yourself we are U.S. agents. Perhaps we are and perhaps not. But if we are—we have certain connections. You need help and we're the best in sight. You don't dare call in your own military. They'd send a ship—maybe—and you'd wonder if it was half bribe hungry and half commie sympathizers. You're on your own. Or you were. Now—you can use us."

Use was the right word. It gave a man like Siauw the idea that he might still walk the tightrope. "You know this Judas, eh?" Siauw asked.

"Yes. Everything I've told you about him is fact." With a few trimmings I've guessed at, Nick thought. "You were surprised to see Tala. Ask her who brought her home. How she arrived."

Siauw turned to Tala. She said, "Mr. Bard brought me home. In a U.S. Navy boat. You can call Adam and you'll see."

Nick admired her quick mind—she wouldn't reveal the submarine unless he did. "But from where?" Siauw asked.

"You cannot expect us to tell you everything while you cooperate with the enemy," Nick replied smoothly. "The facts are she is here. We brought her back."

"But my son—Amir—is he all right?" Siauw was wondering if they had sunk Judas' boat.

"As far as we know. Anyway—you'll know for sure in a few hours. And if he's not, wouldn't you like to have us around? Why don't we all go after Judas?"

Siauw got up and paced the wide porch. Servants in white jackets stiffened at their posts near the doors when he approached. It was not often you saw the big man move like this—worried, thinking hard, like an ordinary man. Suddenly he turned and gave a spatter of orders to an elderly type with a red badge on his spotless coat.

Tala whispered, "He's ordering rooms and dinner. We will stay."

When they retired at ten o'clock Nick tried several subterfuges to get Tala into his room. She was in another wing of the big house. The way was blocked by a number of the white-jackets who never seemed to leave their desk-seats at the intersections of the hallways. He went into Nordenboss' room. "How can we get Tala over here?"

Nordenboss had stripped off his shirt and trousers and lay on the big bed, a mound of muscle and sweat. "What a man," he said wearily. "Can't do without it for one night."

"Dammit—I want her here to cover us when we slip out."

"Oh. We're slipping out?"

"Get near the dock. Watch for Judas and Amir."

"Never mind. I got the word. They are due at the dock in the morning. We might as well get some sleep."

"Why didn't you tell me this before?"

"I just found out. From the son of my man who disappeared."

"The son know who did it?"

"No. My theory is the army. Judas' money got rid of him."

"We have an awful lot of scores to settle with that madman."

"So have a lot of other people."

"We'll do it for them too, if we can. Okay. Let's get up at dawn and take a walk. If we choose to go toward the beach will anybody stop us?"

"I don't think so. I think Siauw will let us watch the whole bit. We're another angle in his games—and man, he sure uses complicated rules."

At the door Nick turned. "Hans—would Colonel Sudirmat's influence reach this far?"

"An interesting question. I've been thinking about it

myself. No. Not his own influence. These local despots are jealous and stay apart. But with money? Yes. As a go-between with some for himself? It could be the way it happened."

"I see. Good night, Hans."

"Good night. And you did a fine job of selling Siauw, Mr. Bard."

An hour before dawn the Portagee ketch *Oporto* raised the light marking the headland south of Loponusias' docks, came about and stood slowly toward sea under a single steadying sail. Bert Geitsch issued crisp orders. Sailors cranked up the hidden davits that swung a big speedy-looking launch overside.

In Judas' cabin Muller and Nife shared a pot of tea and glasses of schnapps with their leader. Nife was excited. He fingered his half-hidden knives. The others hid their amusement at him, showing the tolerance one might for a retarded child. Unfortunately—but he *was* a member of the family, you might say. And Nife was useful for especially nasty jobs.

Judas said, "The procedure is the same. You lay two hundred yards offshore and they bring out the money. Siauw and two men—no more, in their boat. You show him the boy. Let them talk a moment. They toss over the money. You leave. Now there may be trouble. This new agent Al Bard may try something stupid. If anything looks wrong, get away."

"They can take us," observed Muller, always the practical tactician. "We have a machine gun and a bazooka. They can equip one of their company launches with heavy firepower and swoop out from a dock. For that matter they could put a piece of artillery in any of their buildings and—blam!"

"But they won't," Judas purred. "Have you forgotten your history so quickly, my dear friend? For ten years we imposed our will and the victims loved us for it. They even delivered rebels to us themselves. Men will take any amount of oppression if it is logically exercised. But let us say they *do* come out and tell you, 'Look! We have an 88mm. gun trained on you from that warehouse. Surrender!' You strike your colors, old friend, as meek as lambs. And within twenty-four hours I'll have you out of their hands again. You know you can trust me—and you can guess how I would do it."

"Yes." Muller tilted his head toward a cabinet containing Judas' radio equipment. Every other day Judas made brief coded contact with a vessel of the rapidly growing Chicom Navy, sometimes a submarine, usually a corvette or other surface ship. It was comforting to think of that terrific firepower backing you up. Hidden reserves; or as the old general staff used to say, *be more than you seem.*

There was danger in it, too, Muller knew. He and Judas were robbing the Chicoms of the dragon's share of ransom moneys, and sooner or later they would be found out and the claws would thrust at them. He hoped when that happened they would be long gone, with handsome funds for themselves and Odessa's treasury—the international fund on which ex-Nazis draw. Muller prided himself on loyalty.

Judas poured their second schnapps with a smile. He guessed what Muller was thinking. His own loyalty was not as passionate. Muller did not know that the Chinese had warned him he could only expect help, if he got in trouble, at their discretion. And often the every-other-day contacts were sent up in the air. He received no answer— but he told Muller he did. And one thing he had discovered. When he made radio contact he could tell whether it was with a sub or a surface ship that had high antennas and a strong broad signal. It was a scrap of information that might somehow become valuable.

The golden arc of the sun was peeping over the horizon as Judas waved good-by to Muller, Nife and Amir. The

Loponusias heir was handcuffed, a sturdy Japanese AB was at the tiller.

Judas returned to his cabin and poured himself a third schnapps before he put the bottle back with finality. The rule was two—but he felt elated. *Mein Gott* how the money rolled in! He downed the drink and went on deck and stretched and breathed deeply. A cripple, was he?

"Honorable scars!" he exclaimed in English.

He went below and unlocked a cabin where three young Chinese girls, none over fifteen, greeted him with tittery smiles to mask their fear and hatred. He looked at them impassively. He had bought them from peasant families on Penghu as diversion for himself and the crew, but he knew each one so well now that he was bored with them. They behaved—controlled with big promises that need never be kept. He shut the door and locked it.

In front of the cabin in which Tala was imprisoned he stopped thoughtfully. Why in hell not? He deserved it and he intended to have her sooner or later. He held out his hand for the key, took it from the guard, and went in and closed the door.

The slim shape on the narrow bunk excited him more. A virgin? Probably—those families were strict, although the naughty little girls skipped around on these immoral tropical islands and you never could be really sure.

"Hello, Tala." He put a hand on a fine-boned leg and ran it slowly upward.

"Hello." The reply was muffled. She kept her face toward the bulkhead.

His hand squeezed a thigh, fondled the round rump and explored crevices. What a hard, strong-fleshed body she had! Little bundles of muscles like cordage. Not an ounce of fat on her. He inserted his hand under the blue pajama top and his own flesh quivered delightfully as his fingers caressed warm, smooth skin.

She rolled further onto her stomach to avoid him as he tried to reach her breasts. He breathed faster and saliva poured onto his tongue as he imagined them—round and hard as little rubber balls? Or say—ovaled a little like ripe fruit on a vine?

"Be nice to me, Tala," he said as she evaded his probing hand with another twist. "You can have anything you want. And soon you'll go home. Sooner if you're nice."

She was as wiry as an eel. He reached, she writhed away. Trying to hold her was like grabbing a lean, scared puppy. He threw himself onto the rim of the bunk and she used leverage against the bulkhead to pry him away. He fell to the floor. He got up, swore and ripped the pajama top from her. He got only a quick look as they struggled in the dim light—hardly any breasts at all! *Ach*—that was all right, he enjoyed lean ones.

He rammed her against the wall and again she braced herself against the bulkhead, thrust with her arms and legs, and he slid off the edge.

"Enough," he roared as he staggered up. He grabbed a handful of pajama pants and ripped them down. The cotton tore away, transformed into rags in his hands. He got both hands on a thrashing leg and dragged her half off the bunk, fending off the other leg which kicked at his head.

"A boy!" he yelled. His astonishment relaxed his grip for an instant and a hard foot caught him in the chest and bounced him across the narrow cabin. He recovered his balance and waited. The boy on the bunk gathered himself like a coiling snake—watching—waiting.

"So," Judas growled. "You're Akim Machmur."

"Some day I'll kill you," the youth snarled.

"How did you exchange places with your sister?"

"I'll cut you into many pieces."

"It was at the payoff! That fool Muller. But how—how?"

Judas studied the boy. Even with his face contorted with a killing rage you could see that Akim was the exact image of Tala. It would not be difficult to fool someone under the right conditions—

"Tell me," Judas roared. "It was when you went in the boat to Fong Island to get the money, wasn't it? Did Muller dock?"

A giant bribe? He would kill Muller personally. No. Muller was treacherous but no fool. He had heard a rumor that Tala was home, but he had thought it was a Machmur ruse to cover the fact that she was a prisoner.

Judas cursed and feinted with his good arm, the one grown so powerful with use it had the strength of two ordinary limbs. Akim ducked and the real blow connected and swept him into the corner of the bunk with a brutal crash. Judas plucked him up and slammed him again, using only the one hand. It made him feel powerful to keep his other arm, with its hook and tensile claw and small built-in pistol barrel, behind him. He could handle *any* man with one hand behind him! The satisfying thought cooled some of his wrath. Akim lay in a crumpled heap. Judas went out and slammed the door.

Chapter 6

THE sea was smooth and bright as Muller lounged in the motor launch, watching the Loponusias' docks grow larger. There were several ships at the long jetties, including Adam Machmur's pretty yacht and a good-size diesel workboat. Muller chuckled. You could hide a big weapon in any of the buildings and blow them out of the water or force them to land. But they wouldn't dare. He relished the feeling of power.

He saw a clump of people at the landward end of the largest pier. Someone went down the ramp to the floating dock where a small cabin cruiser was tied up. They would probably come out in her. He would follow orders. Once he had disobeyed them, but it had all come out okay. At Fong Island they ordered him to come in, using a bullhorn. Mindful of artillery he had obeyed, ready to threaten them with reprisals, but they had explained that their powerboat would not start.

In fact he had enjoyed the feeling of authority as Adam Machmur had handed him the money. When one of the Machmur sons tearfully embraced his sister he had magnanimously let them chat for a few moments while he assured Adam that his daughter would be returned as soon as the third payment was made and certain political matters settled.

"You have my word as an officer and gentleman," he had promised Machmur. The brown-faced fool. Machmur had given him three bottles of fine brandy and they had cemented the pledge with a quick glass.

But he wouldn't do it again. The Japanese AB had extracted a bottle and a packet of yen for his "friendship" silence. And Nife hadn't been along. You could never trust *him,* with his worship of Judas. Muller glanced distastefully to where Nife sat cleaning his nails with a shining blade, peeking at Amir every little while to see if the boy watched. The youth ignored him. Even in handcuffs, Muller thought, the lad could undoubtedly swim like a fish.

"Nife," he ordered, handing over the key, "secure those cuffs around athwart."

From a porthole of the workboat Nick and Nordenboss watched the launch pass shoreward, then throttle down and begin to circle slowly.

"The boy is there," Hans said. "And that's Muller and Nife. I've never seen the Jap sailor before but he's probably the one who came in with them at Machmur's."

Nick was clad only in swimming trunks. His clothes, the reworked Luger he called Wilhelmina and the blade, Hugo, which he usually wore strapped to his forearm, were hidden in a nearby seat locker. With them, in his shorts, was his other standard weapon—the deadly gas pellet, Pierre.

"You're real light cavalry now," Hans said. "Are you sure you want to go out without a weapon?"

"Siauw will have a fit as it is. If we do any damage he'll never accept the deal we want to make."

"I'll be covering you. I can score all right at this distance."

"Don't. Unless I'm dead."

Hans shuddered. You didn't develop many friendships in this business—it hurt to even think of losing one.

Hans peered from a forward porthole. "The cruiser is coming out. Give it two minutes and they'll be busy with each other."

"Right. Remember the arguments for Siauw if we bring it off."

Nick went up the ladder and crouched low as he crossed the small deck and slipped noiselessly into the water between the workboat and the dock. He swam around the bow. The launch and the cabin cruiser were approaching each other. The launch throttled down, the cruiser slowed. He heard clutches disengage. He filled and deflated his lungs several times.

They were two hundred yards from him. The dredged channel looked about ten feet deep but the water was clear and transparent. You could see small fish. He hoped they didn't see him coming, for there was no chance of his being mistaken for a shark.

The men on the two small boats were looking at each other and starting to talk. The cruiser held Siauw, a small sailor at the controls on the little flying bridge and a tough-looking aide of Siauw's called Abdul.

Nick lowered his head, swam down until he was just above the bottom, and measured his powerful strokes as he watched small patches of shell and weed to hold a straight course, sighting ahead from one to another. As part of his job Nick stayed in top physical condition with a regimen worthy of an Olympic athlete. Even with frequent odd hours, alcohol and unexpected foods, if you put your mind to it you could follow a reasonable program. You dodged the third drink, selected mostly proteins when you ate, and slept extra hours when you could. Nick did not cheat—it was his life insurance.

He concentrated much of his training, of course, on combat skills, yoga and many sports, including swimming, golf and tumbling.

Now he swam calmly until he estimated he was close to the boats. He rolled onto his side, saw the two oval boat shapes against the brighter sky and let himself come up at the bow of the launch, reasonably sure its occupants were looking over the stern. Hidden by the swell of the boat's lapstreak side, he discovered he was invisible to anyone except people who might be well out on the pier. He heard voices above him.

"Are you sure you're all right?" That was Siauw.

"Yes." Perhaps Amir?

Gutteral. That would be Muller. "We mustn't drop that nice package into the water. Come alongside slowly—use a little power—no, don't heave a line—I don't want to make fast."

The cruiser's engine purred. The launch's propeller was not turning, her engine idled. Nick surface-dived, looked up, sighted, and with powerful sweeps of his big arms came up at the lowest point of the launch's side, hooking one mighty hand on the wooden coaming.

It was more than enough. He got a grip with his other hand and in an instant had a leg over the side like an acrobat doing a hock mount. He landed on deck, sweeping hair and water out of his eyes, a wary and alert Neptune popped from the depths to face his foes.

Muller, Nife and the Japanese sailor were all near the stern. Nife moved first and Nick thought he was quite slow—or perhaps he compared his own perfect vision and reflexes against the handicaps of surprise and morning schnapps. Nick sprang before the knife cleared its case. His palm shot up under Nife's chin and as his legs caught on the boat's sides Nife jackknifed backwards into the water as if yanked by a cord.

Muller was fast with a gun, although he was an old man by comparison with the others. He had always secretly enjoyed Western movies and he carried a 7.65mm. Mauser in a belt holster partly cut away. But it had a safety strap and the automatic's safety was on. Muller made his fastest try, but Nick plucked the weapon out of his hand while it was still pointed at the deck. He pushed Muller into a heap.

The Japanese sailor was the most interesting of the trio. He swung a backhand edge-of-hand slash at Nick's throat which would have laid him down for ten minutes if it had landed on his Adam's apple. Holding Muller's gun in his right hand, he made a ramp with his left forearm with his own fist near his forehead. The sailor's blow was guided up into the air and Nick poked him in the nose with his elbow.

Through the tears that clouded his eyes the sailor's expression showed surprise chased by fear. He was no black belt expert but he knew professionalism when he saw it. But—perhaps just an accident! What a reward if he dropped the big white man. He fell on the rail, hooked his arms over it, and his legs flashed at Nick—one for the crotch and one for the belly like twin kicks of a mule.

Nick faded aside. He could have turn-blocked but he didn't want the bruises those strong, hard-muscled legs could give him. He caught the highest ankle with an underhand scoop, locked on it, lifted—turned—flipped the sailor into a clumsy huddle against the rail. Nick stepped back one pace, still holding the Mauser in one hand with a finger through the trigger guard.

The sailor straightened, slumped back, hanging by one arm. Muller was struggling to his feet. Nick kicked his left ankle and he collapsed again. He said to the sailor, "Stop it or I'll finish you."

The man nodded his head. Nick leaned over and removed his belt knife and tossed it overboard.

"Who has the key to the boy's handcuffs?"

The sailor gasped, looked at Muller, said nothing. Muller pushed himself erect again, looking stunned. "Give me the key to the handcuffs," Nick said.

Muller hesitated, then produced it from the pocket of

his white ducks. "This will do you no good, you fool. We are—"

"Sit down and shut up or I'll knock you down again."

Nick unlocked Amir from the thwart and gave him the key so that he could free his other wrist. "Thank you. Thank you. Thank you—"

"Listen to your father," Nick said to stop him.

Siauw was yelling orders, threats, and what were probably oaths in three or four languages. The cruiser had drifted about fifteen feet from the launch. Nick reached over the side and pulled Nife aboard and stripped him of his armament as if plucking a chicken. Nife grabbed for the Mauser and Nick chopped him beside the head with his other hand. A moderate blow but it put Nife down at the feet of the Jap sailor.

"Hey," Nick yelled at Siauw. "Hey—" Siauw sputtered to silence. "Don't you want your son back? Here he is."

"You'll die for this!" Siauw yelled in English. "Nobody asked for your goddam interference!" He shouted commands in Indonesian at the two men with him, at the men on the dock.

Nick said to Amir. "You want to go back to Judas?"

"I'll die first. Get behind me. He's telling Abdul Nono to shoot you. They've got rifles in the scale house and they are good shots."

The slim youth deliberately moved between Nick and the shore buildings. He called to his father. "I won't go back. Don't shoot. This man is for us."

Siauw looked as if he might explode like a balloon filled with hydrogen brought near a flame. But he was silent.

"Who are you?" Amir asked.

"They say I'm an American agent. Anyway—I want to help you. We can take the ship and free the others. Your father and the other families don't agree. What do you say?"

"I say fight." Amir's face glowed, then dulled as he added, "But they will be hard to convince."

Nife and the sailor were crawling erect. "Handcuff those two to each other," Nick said. Let the boy feel a victory. Amir put the irons on the men as if he enjoyed doing it.

"Let them go," Siauw called.

"We must fight," Amir answered. "I'm not going back. You don't understand these people. They will kill us all anyway. You cannot buy them." He switched to Indonesian and exchanged bursts of argument with his father. It had to be argument, Nick decided—with all those gestures and explosive sounds.

After awhile Amir turned to Nick. "I think he is convinced just a little. He is going to talk with his guru."

"His *what?*"

"His counselor. His—I don't know the word in English. You can say religious advisor but it's more like—"

"His psychiatrist?" Nick provided the word partly as a disgusted joke.

"Yes, in a way! The man who guides his life."

"Oh, brother." Nick checked the Mauser and slipped it into the waistband of his trunks. "All right—herd those guys forward and I'll take this tub in to shore."

Hans talked to Nick while he showered and dressed. There was no hurry—Siauw had scheduled a meeting in three hours. Muller, Nife and the sailor had been taken away by Siauw's men and Nick had felt it wisest not to protest.

"We're in a bunch of hornets," Hans said. "I thought Amir could convince his father. Return of the beloved progeny. He really loves the boy but he still thinks he can do business with Judas. I think he has phoned some of the other families and they agree."

Nick was strapping on Hugo. Wouldn't Nife like to add this stiletto to his collection? It was made of the finest steel obtainable. "It seems to run up and down the line, Hans. Even the big shots have been bowing their necks so long they'd rather connive than face a clash. They'll have to change fast or the twentieth-century types like Judas will chew them up and spit them out. What's this guru like?"

"His name is Buduk. Some of these gurus are splendid men. Scholars. Theologians. Real psychologists and so on. Then there are the Buduks."

"He's a thief?"

"He's a politician."

"You answered my question."

"He's got it made here. The rich man's philosopher with extra intuition he gets from the spirit world. You know the jazz. I never trusted him, but the reason I know he's phoney is because little Abu slipped me the word. Our holy man is a secret swinger when he slips away to Djakarta."

"Can I see him?"

"I think so. I'll ask."

"Go ahead."

Hans returned in ten minutes. "Sure. I'll take you to him. Siauw is still mad. He practically spat at me."

They followed an interminable winding path under thick trees to the small, neat house occupied by Buduk. Most of the native houses huddled together, but the sage apparently required seclusion. He greeted them seated cross-legged on cushions in a clean, barren room. Hans introduced Nick and Buduk nodded impassively, "I have heard much about Mr. Bard and the problem."

"Siauw says he wants your advice," Nick said bluntly.

"I suggest he resists. He believes he can negotiate."

"Violence is never a good solution."

"Peace is best," Nick agreed smoothly. "But would you call a man a fool if he sat still in front of a tiger?"

"Sit still? You mean patience. And then the gods may tell the tiger to go away."

"What if we hear a loud hungry rumble from the tiger's belly?"

Buduk frowned. Nick guessed that his clientele rarely argued with him. The old boy was slow. Buduk said, "I will meditate and give my suggestions."

"If you suggest that we be brave, that we must fight because we will win, I would be very grateful."

"I hope my counsel pleases you as well as Siauw and the powers of earth and sky."

"Counsel fight," Nick said softly, "and there will be three thousand dollars awaiting you. In Djakarta or anywhere you want it. In gold or any *way* you like it." He heard Hans gasp. It wasn't the amount—for an operation of this type it was a trifle. Hans thought he was too blunt.

Buduk didn't bat an eye. "Your generosity is surprising. With such money I could do much good."

"Is it agreed?"

"Only the gods will tell. I will answer at the meeting very soon."

On the way back along the path Hans said, "Nice try. You surprised me. But I guess it's best to get it out into the open."

"He didn't go along."

"I think you're right. He's out to hang us."

"He's either working directly for Judas or he's got such a racket going here he doesn't want to rock the boat. He's like the families—his spine is a piece of wet macaroni."

"Have you wondered why we're not guarded?"

"I can guess. We wouldn't get a mile?"

"Right. I heard Siauw issuing orders."

"Can you get Tala in to see us?"

"I think so. See you at the room in a few minutes."

It took longer than a few minutes, but Nordenboss returned with Tala. She came straight to Nick and held his arm and looked into his eyes. "I saw. I hid in a shed. The way you rescued Amir was wonderful."

"Have you talked to him?"

"No. His father has kept him with him. They were arguing."

"Amir wants to resist?"

"Well—he did. But if you heard Siauw—"

"Plenty of pressure?"

"Obedience is such a habit with us."

Nick drew her to a couch. "Tell me about Buduk. I'm sure he is against us. He will advise Siauw to send Amir back with Muller and the others."

Tala lowered her dark eyes. "I hope it is no worse."

"How could it be?"

"You have embarrassed Siauw. Buduk may permit him to punish you. This meeting—it will be a big thing. Did you know that? Since everyone knows what you have done and it was against both Siauw and Buduk's wishes there is—well, a matter of face."

"My god! Now it's *face*."

"Rather Buduk's gods. Their faces and his."

Hans chuckled. "Glad we're not on the island to the north. They eat you up there, Al. Broiled with onion and sauces."

"Very funny."

Hans sighed. "Come to think of it—not so funny."

Nick asked Tala, "Siauw was willing to withhold final judgment about resisting for a few days until I grabbed Muller and the others, then he got all upset even though he has his son back. Why? He turns to Buduk. Why? Amir is softening up according to what I can figure. Why? Buduk refused a bribe although I hear he takes. Why?"

"People," Tala said sadly.

The one word reply puzzled Nick. People? "Sure—people. But what are the angles? This deal is developing into a regular cobweb of reasons—"

"Let me try to explain, Mr. Bard," Hans interjected smoothly. "Even with the useful idiocy of the masses, rulers have to be careful. They learn to use power but cater to emotions and above all to what we can laughingly call public opinion. Are you with me?"

"Your irony comes through," Nick answered. "Go on."

"If six determined people turned against a Napoleon or a Hitler or a Stalin or Franco—poof!"

"Poof?"

"If they have *real* determination. To put a bullet or a knife in a despot without regard for their own death."

"All right. I buy that."

"But these conniving types not only prevent a half-dozen making a decision—they control hundreds of thousands—millions! You can't do it with a gun on your hip. But it's done! So subtly that poor fools burn *themselves* up as an example instead of getting next to the dictator at a party and shoving a shiv in his gut."

"Granted. Although it would take a few months or years to worm your way next to the big shot."

"What's that if you are really determined? But the leaders have to keep them so confused they never develop such purpose. How is it done? By controlling the mass of people. Never let 'em think. So to your questions to Tala. Siauw let us stay to play the angles. See if there was a way to use us against Judas—and ride with the winner. You went into action in front of a few dozen of his people, and the word of it is halfway across his little kingdom by now. You got his son back. People wonder why he didn't do it? They may figure out how he and the rich families played along. The rich call it wise tactics. The poor may call it cowardice. The people have simple principles. Amir softens up? I can imagine what his father is telling him about his duty to the dynasty. Buduk? He would take anything that's not red hot if he didn't have a pot holder or gloves. He'd have asked you for more than three thousand, and gotten it I suppose, but he knows—intuitively or practically, just as Siauw does—they have the *people* to impress."

Nick rubbed his head. "Maybe you follow this, Tala. Is he right?"

Her soft lips pouted close to his cheek as if she pitied

his slow wit. "Yes. When you see thousands of the people gathered at the temple you will understand."

"What temple?"

"Where the meeting with Buduk and the others will be held and he will make his suggestions."

Hans added cheerfully, "It's a very old structure. Magnificent. They used to have human barbecues there a century or so ago. And trials by combat. The people aren't so dumb about some things. They'd draw up their armies and let two champions fight it out. Similar to the Mediterranean practice. David and Goliath. It was the most popular entertainment. Like the Roman games. Real action with real blood—"

"Issue challenges and all that?"

"Yes. The big shots had it rigged so that only their professional scrappers could be challenged. After awhile the citizens learned to keep their mouths shut. The great champion, Saadi in the last century, killed ninety-two men in individual combat."

Tala brightened. "He was invincible."

"How did *he* die?"

"An elephant stepped on him. He was only forty."

"I'd say the elephant was invincible," Nick said gloomily. "Why haven't they disarmed us, Hans?"

"You'll see—at the temple."

Amir and three armed men arrived at Nick's room, "to show them the way."

The Loponusias heir was apologetic. "Thank you for what you did for me. I hope everything—works out."

Nick said bluntly, "Looks as if some of the fight has been taken out of you."

Amir flushed and turned to Tala. "You shouldn't be alone with these strangers."

"I'll be alone with whom I please."

"You need an injection, boy," Nick said. "Half guts and half brains."

It took Amir an instant to understand. His hand went to the big kris in his belt. Nick said, "Forget it. Your Dad wants us." He went out the door leaving Amir red and glaring.

They walked for nearly a mile through the twisting paths, past Buduk's spacious grounds, into a meadow-like plain hidden by giant trees that made the sun-washed building in the center stand out impressively. It was a giant, eye-stopping hybrid of architecture and statuary. A blend of centuries of interwoven religions. The dominant structure was a two-story high Buddha-like figure with a golden cap.

"Is that real gold?" Nick asked.

"Yes," Tala answered. "There are many jewels inside. They are guarded day and night by the holy ones."

"I wasn't planning to steal them," Nick said.

In front of the statue was a wide, permanent reviewing stand now occupied by a number of men, and on the plain in front of them was a solid mass of people. Nick tried to guess—eight thousand—nine? And more pouring in from the rim of the field like ribbons of ants from the forests. There were armed men flanking the reviewing stand, and some of the people seemed grouped, as if they were special clubs, bands or dancing teams. "They drew all these in three hours?" he asked Tala.

"Yes."

"Wow. Tala—whatever happens stay near me to interpret and talk for me. And don't be afraid to speak loud."

She squeezed his arm. "I'll help if I can."

A voice boomed over a public address system. "Mr. Nordenboss—Mr. Bard—please join us on the sacred steps."

Plain wooden seats had been saved for them. Muller, Nife and the Japanese sailor sat a few yards away. There were plenty of guards and they looked tough.

Siauw and Buduk took turns at the microphone. Tala explained—her tones more and more dejected, "Siauw says you betrayed his hospitality and ruined his plans. Amir was sort of a business hostage for a project of benefit to all."

"He would have made a great pretzel twister," Nick growled.

"Buduk says Muller and the others are to be freed with apologies." She gasped as Buduk rattled on. "And—"

"What?"

"You and Nordenboss are to be sent with them. As payment for our impoliteness."

Siauw replaced Buduk at the mike. Nick stood up, held Tala by the hand and forced his way to Siauw. Forced—because by the time he covered the twenty feet two guards were hanging on his arms. Nick called on his small store of Indonesian and bellowed, "Bung Loponusias—I want to speak of your son, Amir. About the handcuffs. About his courage."

Siauw gestured angrily to the guards. They yanked. Nick twisted his arms toward their thumbs and broke their grips easily. They grabbed again. He did it again. The roar from the crowd was amazing. It flooded over them like the first wind of a hurricane.

"I speak of courage," Nick yelled. "Amir has courage!"

The crowd screamed enthusiastically. More! Excitement! Anything! Let the *Orang America* talk. Or kill him. But let's not go back to work. Tapping rubber trees doesn't look like hard work, but it is.

Nick got a hand around the microphone and yelled, "Amir is brave! I can tell you all!"

This was something like it! The crowd whooped and roared with the mass reaction of all crowds when you needle their emotions. Siauw motioned the guards away. Nick held up both hands above his head as if he knew he could speak. It took a minute for the cacophony to subside.

Siauw said in English, "You have said it. Now please sit down." He would have had Nick dragged away, but the American had caught the attention of the crowd. It could turn to sympathy in an instant. Siauw had been handling crowds all his life. Wait—

"Please come here," Nick called and waved to Amir.

The youth joined Nick and Tala, looking confused. First this Al Bard insulted him, now he praised him to the people. The thunder of acclamation was pleasant.

Nick said to Tala—"now translate this loud and clear —"

"The man Muller has insulted Amir. Let Amir regain his honor—"

Tala shouted the words at the mike.

Nick went on and the girl echoed him, "Muller is old ... but he has his champion with him ... the man with the knives ... Amir demands a test ..."

Amir whispered, "I cannot demand a test. Only champions fight for—"

Nick said, "And since Amir cannot fight ... I offer myself as his champion! Let Amir regain his honor ... let us *all* regain *our* honor."

The crowd cared little about honor but a great deal about spectacles and excitement. Their howls were louder than before.

Siauw knew when he was whipped—but he appeared self-satisfied as he said to Nick, "You have made it necessary. All right. Take off your clothes."

Tala was pulling at Nick's arm. He turned, surprised to find her in tears. "No—no," she cried. "The challenger fights without weapons. He will kill you."

Nick gulped. "So that's why the ruler's champion always won." His admiration for Saadi dropped to zero. Those ninety-two setups were victims, not challengers.

Amir said, "I don't understand you, Mr. Bard, but I don't think I want to see you killed. Maybe I can get you a chance to run for it."

Nick saw Muller and Nife and the Japanese sailor laughing. Nife waved his biggest knife suggestively and did a hopping dance. The cheers of the crowd vibrated the stands. Nick thought of a picture of a Roman slave he had seen fighting a fully armed soldier with a club. He had pitied the underdog. The poor slave had no choice—he had drawn his pay and sworn to do his duty.

He peeled off his shirt and the shouts reached a crescendo that was hard on the ears. "No, Amir. We'll try our luck."

"You will probably die."

"There's always a chance for a break."

"Look." Amir pointed at a forty-foot square which was being rapidly cleared in front of the temple. "That's the combat square. It hasn't been used in twenty years. It will be swept and clear. No chance for you to use a trick like throwing dirt in his eyes. If you jump out of the square to grab a weapon the guards have a right to kill you."

Nick sighed and removed his shoes. "Now you tell me."

Chapter 7

SIAUW made one more attempt to enforce Buduk's decision without the contest, but his cautious orders were drowned in the din. The crowd yelled as Nick stripped off Wilhelmina and Hugo and gave them to Hans. They roared again when Nife swiftly stripped and hopped down into the arena, carrying his large knife. He looked wiry, well-muscled and alert.

"Think you can handle him?" Hans asked.

"I did until I heard about the rule that only the challenged use weapons. What a con game the old rulers ran—"

"If he gets to you I'll put a slug in him and get your Luger to you somehow, but I don't think we'll live long. Siauw has several hundred soldiers right in this field."

"If he gets to me you won't get him in time to do me much good."

Nick took a deep breath. Tala held his arm, her grip tight with nervous tension. Nick knew more about local customs than he had revealed—his reading and research had been thorough. The customs were a blend of animistic holdovers, Buddhism and Mohammedanism. But this was a moment of truth he could not think of an angle for—

except to whip Nife, and that would not be simple. The system was rigged for the house.

The crowd became impatient. They grumbled, then roared cheerfully again as Nick stepped carefully down the wide steps, his muscles rippling under his tan. He smiled and raised a hand like a favorite entering a ring.

Siauw, Buduk, Amir, and half-a-dozen armed men who appeared to be officers in Siauw's forces climbed on a low platform overlooking the cleared oblong in which Nife strutted. Nick stayed cautiously outside for a moment. He did not want to step over the low wooden rim—like a polo-field barrier—and perhaps give Nife a chance for a sucker punch attack. A burly man in green pants and shirt, wearing a turban and carrying a gilt mace, came from the temple, bowed to Siauw and entered the ring. The referee, Nick thought, and followed.

The burly man waved Nife to one side of himself, Nick to the other, then waved his arms and stepped back—well back. His meaning was unmistakable. Round one.

Nick balanced on the balls of his feet, his hands out and open, fingers together, thumbs out. This was it. No more thoughts except about what was in front of him. Concentrate. Act. React.

Nife was fifteen feet from him. The wiry, supple Mindanaoan looked fit—perhaps not as fit as himself, but his knife was a rugged ace to top. To Nick's amazement Nife grinned—a white-toothed grimace of pure evil and cruelty—then twisted the handle of the Bowie-type knife in his hand, and a moment later faced Nick with another smaller dagger in his left hand!

Nick did not glance at the burly referee. He kept his attention on his opponent. They were not likely to call any fouls around here. Nife crouched and came forward, light-footed . . . and thus began one of the strangest, most exciting and amazing contests that ever took place in the ancient arena.

For a long time Nick concentrated only on evasion of

those deadly blades and the fast-moving man who wielded them. Nife rushed—Nick bounded back, to the left past the shorter blade. Nife grinned his demonic grimace and charged again. Nick feinted to the left and sprang away to the right.

Nife chuckled evilly and turned smoothly, following his prey. Let the big man play for awhile—it added to the fun. He spread his blades a little wider and advanced more slowly. Nick evaded the small blade with an inch to spare. Next time, he knew, Nife would allow for those inches with an extra lunge.

Nick covered twice the ground his adversary used, taking advantage of the full forty feet, yet making sure he had at least fifteen or so feet in which to maneuver. Nife charged. Nick faded back, moved to the right, and this time with a lightning tap at the end of a lunge with his arm like a fencer without a blade, tipped Nife's hand aside and jumped into the clear.

The crowd loved it at first, greeting every attack and defensive move with a storm of yells, cheers and whoops. Then, as Nick continued to retreat and dodge, they became bloodthirsty from their own excitement and their cheers were for Nife. Nick couldn't understand them, but the tones were self-evident—*cut his guts out!*

Nick used another fencing riposte to divert Nife's right hand and when he reached the other end of the ring he turned and grinned at Nife and waved a hand at the crowd. That caught their fancy. The roars sounded like cheers again—but not for long.

The sun was hot. Sweat poured over Nick but he was pleased to discover he was not breathing hard. Nife was dripping perspiration and he was starting to puff. The schnapps was telling on him. He paused and flipped the small knife over into a throwing hold. The crowd screamed with delight. They didn't stop when Nife tossed the blade back into a fighting grip, edge up and made a stabbing motion with it as if to say—"you think I'm crazy? I won't throw one away, I'll butcher him."

He rushed. Nick went low, parried and got away under the big blade, which nicked his biceps and drew blood. A woman shrieked happily.

Nife came after him slowly, like a boxer cornering his adversary. He matched Nick's feints. Left, right, left. Nick flashed forward, got a brief hold on the right wrist, evading the larger blade by a fraction of an inch, and spun Nife around and jumped on past him before he could bring the smaller knife around. He knew it had missed his kidneys by less than the length of a ball-point pen. Nife almost fell, caught himself and rushed angrily after his victim. Nick hopped aside, delivered a *savate* kick under the small blade that caught Nife above the knee but did little damage as Nick tumbled over in a side somersault and leaped away.

The Mindanaoan was intent on business now. This jack-in-the-box was a bigger handful than he had imagined he might be. He stalked Nick carefully, and on his next lunge sliced a deep furrow in Nick's thigh as he dodged. Nick felt nothing—that would come later.

He thought that Nife was slowing a little. Certainly he was breathing much harder. Now was the time. Nife came in smoothly, blades fairly wide, intent on cornering his foe. Nick let him have ground, backing toward a corner in small jumps. Nife knew a moment of elation as he thought that Nick could not escape him this time—and then Nick leaped straight forward into him, parrying both Nife's arms with quick jabs of his hands formed into stiff-fingered judo spears.

Nife opened his arms and came back with the thrusts which should spit his prey on both blades. Nick went under the right arm and slid his own left hand up it, not going away this time but coming up behind Nife, thrusting his left arm up and in back of Nife's neck—following it with his right from the other side to apply an old-fashioned half nelson!

The combatants crashed to the ground, Nife on his face on the hard-packed ground with Nick fastened to his back. Nife's arms were forced up, but he held the blades firmly. Nick had practiced personal combat all his life, and he had been through this particular throw and hold many times. In four or five seconds Nife would discover that he should skewer his opponent by twisting his arms *down*.

Nick applied the headlock with all his force. If you were lucky you could disable or finish your man this way. His grip slipped, his locked hands slid up and over Nife's oily bull neck. Grease! Nick felt it and smelled it. That was what Buduk had done when he gave Nife his brief blessing!

Nife thrashed under him, twisted, a knife-arm crawled backward along the ground. Nick whipped his arms free and got in one pounding fist-chop on the back of Nife's neck as he sprang clear, barely avoiding the shining steel which flashed at him like a viper's fang.

Jumping clear and crouching, Nick studied his man. The neck blow had done some damage. Nife had lost a lot of his bounce. He swayed a little, puffing.

Nick took a deep breath and steadied his muscles, attuned his reflexes. He recalled MacPherson's "orthodox" defense against a trained knife man—"a lightning kick to the testicles or run." MacPherson's manual had never even mentioned what to do against two knives!

Nife stepped forward, stalking Nick cautiously now—carrying the blades wider and low. Nick retreated, faded left, dodged right, then sprang forward using a hand-parry to tilt the shorter blade aside as it swept upward at his groin. Nife tried to pull his blow but before his arm stopped its forward lunge Nick had taken one step forward, spun beside the other and cross-locked the extended arm with the V of his own arm under Nife's elbow and a hand upon the top of Nife's wrist. The arm snapped with a crunching sound.

Even as Nife screamed, Nick's keen eyes saw the big blade make its swing toward him, coming around in front of Nife. He saw it all as clearly as a slow-motion movie. The steel was low and edge-up and due to penetrate just under his navel. There was no way to block, with his arms just completing the snapping of Nife's elbow. There was only—

It all took a small fraction of a second. A man without lightning reflexes, a man who had not taken his training seriously and made an honest effort to stay in condition, would have died right there in a welter of his own intestines and belly flesh.

Nick spun left, carrying Nife's arm as you would for the orthodox fall and lock. He crossed his own right leg forward with a jump, twisting, turning, falling—Nife's blade caught the point of his thigh bone, tore the flesh cruelly, and ripped a long superficial slash in Nick's buttock as he dove forward to the ground, carrying Nife with him.

Nick felt no pain. You don't—*immediately;* Nature gives you fighting time. He made the leg whip across Nife's back and pinned the Mindanaoan's good arm with the leg lock. They lay on the ground, Nife on the bottom, Nick across his back, pinning his arms in the snake-in-the-bow lock. Nife still had his blade in his good arm but it was temporarily useless. Nick had one free arm—but he was not in position to strangle his man, poke out his eyes or grasp his testicles. It was a stand-off—the instant Nick released his hold he could expect a thrust.

It was time for Pierre. With his free hand Nick felt his bleeding rump, pretended pain, groaned. A sigh of blood-identification, moans of sympathy and a few taunting cries, sounded from the crowd. Swiftly Nick took the little pellet out of the hidden slot in his shorts, felt the tiny lever with his thumb. He grimaced and writhed about like a TV wrestler, contorting his features to express horrible pain.

Nife was a great help to the act. As he struggled to get free he wrenched them along the ground like some grotesque eight-limbed squirming crab. Nick pinned Nife down as well as he could, got his hand near the knifelover's nose and released some of Pierre's deadly contents, pretending to grope for the man's throat.

In open air Pierre's swiftly expanding vapor dissipated quickly. It was primarily an indoor weapon. But its fumes were lethal, and for Nife, panting for breath—his face a few inches from the small oval exuder of doom hidden in Nick's palm—there was no escape.

Nick had never held one of Pierre's victims as the gas took effect, and he never wanted to again. There was a moment of frozen inaction, and you thought death had come. Then Nature protested at the killing of an organism she had spent billions of years developing and muscles tightened and there was a last struggle for survival. Nife— or Nife's body—tried to wrench free with more power than the man had used when in command of his senses. He almost threw Nick off. A horrible retching scream burst from his throat and the crowd yowled with him. They thought it was a battle cry.

Many moments later, when Nick stood up slowly and watchfully, Nife's legs jerked fitfully, even though his eyes were wide and staring. The body and Nick were smeared with blood and dirt. Gravely Nick raised both arms to the sky, bent and touched the earth, turned Nife over with a respectful and gentle motion, and closed the eyes. He took a clot of blood from his own buttock and touched his fallen adversary on the forehead, the heart and the stomach. He scraped up a little earth, blotted up more blood, and poked the mess into Nife's sagging mouth—thrusting the spent pellet down the man's throat with his finger.

The crowd adored it. Their primitive emotions were

expressed in a howl of acclaim that shivered the tall trees. Honor thy foe!

Nick stood up, spread his arms wide again as he looked at the sky and intoned, *"Dominus vobiscum."* He looked down and made a circle with his thumb and forefinger, then thrust a thumb upward. He muttered, "Rot quick with the rest of the garbage, you crazy throwback."

The mob poured into the arena and raised him on their shoulders, oblivious to the blood. Some reached for it and touched themselves on the forehead with it, like newcomers daubed after a kill at a foxhunt.

Siauw's dispensary was modern. An efficient native doctor put three neat stitches in Nick's buttock and antiseptic and plaster on his two other cuts.

He found Siauw and Hans on the veranda with a dozen others, including Tala and Amir. Hans said briefly, "Quite a duel."

Nick looked at Siauw. "You've seen that they can be beaten. Will you fight?"

"You don't leave me any choice. Muller has been telling me what Judas will do to us."

"Where is Muller—and the Jap?"

"In our guardhouse. They won't go anywhere."

"Can we use your boats to go after the ship? What armament do you have?"

Amir said, "The junk is disguised as a Portagee trader. They have many large cannons. I will try—but I do not think we can take her or sink her."

"Do you have any aircraft? Bombs?"

"We have two," Siauw said gloomily. "An eight-place flying boat and a biplane for crop work. But I only have hand grenades and some dynamite. You would only scratch them."

Nick nodded thoughtfully. "I will destroy Judas and his ship."

"But the prisoners? The sons of my friends—"

"I will free them first, of course." Nick thought—I hope. "And I will do it far from here, which I think will make you happy."

Siauw nodded. This big *Orang America* probably had a U.S. Navy warship on call. After seeing him whip the man with two knives, you could imagine anything. Nick considered asking Hawk for Navy help, then discarded the idea. By the time State and Defense said no, Judas would have found an angle.

"Hans," Nick said, "let's get ready to leave in an hour. I'm sure Siauw will lend us his flying boat."

They took off into the garish afternoon sun. Nick, Hans, Tala, Amir and a native pilot who seemed to know his job well. Shortly after suction broke the hull free from the clinging sea Nick said to the pilot, "Please make a swing out to sea. Pick up a Portagee trader who can't be far offshore. I just want a look."

They found the *Oporto* in twenty minutes, easing along on the northwest leg of a port tack. Nick drew Amir to a window. "There she is," he said. "Now tell me all about her. Cabins. Armament. Where you were confined. Number of men—"

Tala spoke softly from the next seat. "And perhaps I can help."

Nick turned his gray eyes on her for an instant. They were hard and cold. "I thought you could. And afterward I want you both to draw me plans of her decks. As detailed as you can."

At the sound of the plane's engines Judas retreated under the awning, watching from a hatchway. The flying boat went over him, circled. He frowned. That was Loponusias' ship. His finger strayed toward the battle stations button. He withdrew it. Patience. They might have a message. The launch might have broken down.

The slow craft circled the sailing vessel. Amir and Tala talked rapidly, vying with each other to explain details of the ketch-junk which Nick absorbed and retained like a pail collecting droplets from two spouts. Occasionally he asked a question to spur them on.

He saw no AA equipment, although the youngsters described it. If the concealing nets and panels had fallen he would have had the pilot get away—as fast and evasively as he could. They flew past the ship on both sides, crossed directly over her, circled tightly.

"There's Judas," Amir exclaimed. "See. Back— Now he's hidden by the awning again. Watch the port side after-hatch."

"We've seen what I wanted to," Nick said. He leaned forward and talked into the pilot's ear. "Make one more slow pass. Bow to stern directly over her." The flyer nodded.

Nick rolled down the old-fashioned window. From his case he took Nife's five blades—the big double-Bowie and three throwing knives. When they were four hundred yards from the bow he dumped them overside and yelled to the pilot, "Let's head for Djakarta. Now!"

From his seat aft Hans called, "Not bad with no bomb sight. Those knives all seemed to fall on her somewhere."

Nick sat back in his seat. His rump hurt and the bandage squished when he moved. "They'll collect them and get the idea."

As they approached Djakarta Nick said, "We'll stay here overnight and go on to Fong Island tomorrow. Meet at the airport at eight A.M. sharp. Hans—will you take the pilot home with you so that we won't lose him?"

"Sure."

Nick knew that Tala pouted because she was thinking about where *he* would stay. With Mata Nasut. And she was right, but not precisely for the reasons she had in mind. Hans' pleasant face was impassive. Nick was running this project. He would never tell him how agonized he had been during the fight with Nife. He had sweated and breathed as hard as the combatants, ready every instant to draw his pistol and put a slug in Nife and knowing he could never be fast enough to block a blade and wondering how far they would get through the enraged mob. He sighed. You lived rapidly with "Al Bard."

At Mata's Nick took a hot sponge bath—the large wound was not clotted enough to shower—and napped on the patio. She arrived after eight, greeting him with kisses that turned to tears as she inspected his bandages. He sighed. It was pleasant. She was more beautiful than he remembered her.

"You might have been killed," she sobbed. "I told you—I told you—"

"You told me," he said, holding her tightly. "I think they rather expected me."

There was a long silence. "What happened?" she asked.

He told her the events. Minimizing the battle and omitting only their reconnoitering flight over the ship—about which it was possible she might learn very soon. When he had finished she shuddered, cuddling very close, her perfume a kiss in itself. "Thank heaven it wasn't worse. Now you can turn Muller and the sailor over to the police and it's all over."

"Not quite. I'm going to have them sent down to the Machmurs'. It's Judas' turn to pay ransom. His hostages for them if he wants them back."

"Oh, no! You'll be in more danger—"

"It's the name of the game, darling."

"Don't be foolish." Her lips were soft and inventive. Her hands a surprise. "Stay here. Rest. Perhaps now he will go away."

"Perhaps—"

He returned her caresses. There was something about action, even near-disaster, even combat that left wounds, that stimulated him. A return to the primitive, as if you captured your loot and women? He felt a little ashamed and uncivilized—but Mata's butterfly touches rechanneled his thoughts.

She touched the bandage on his buttock. "Does it hurt?"

"Hardly at all."

"We can be careful—"

"Yes—"

She enveloped him like a warm, soft coverlet.

They landed at Fong Island to find Adam Machmur and Gan Bik waiting on the ramp. Nick had a farewell word with Siauw's pilot. "After the ship is serviced you'll be going home to pick up the man Muller and the Japanese sailor. You won't be able to make that roundtrip today, will you?"

"I might if we wanted to risk a night landing here. But I'd rather not." The flyer was a bright-faced young man who spoke English like a man who appreciated it as the international air control language and didn't want to make any mistakes. "If I could return in the morning it would be better, I think. But—" His shrug said he would if he had to. He took orders. He reminded Nick of Gan Bik—he went along because he was not yet sure how much he could buck the system.

"Do it the safe way," Nick said. "Take off as early in the morning as you can."

Teeth flashed like small piano keys against rubbed oak. Nick gave him a sheaf of rupee notes. "That's for a good trip down here. If you pick up those men and get them back to me there'll be four times as much waiting for you."

"It will be done if it can be done, Mr. Bard."

"Things may have changed back there. Buduk is in their pay, I think."

The flyer frowned. "I'll do my best, but if Siauw says no—"

"If you get them, remember they're tough men. Even

handcuffed they can give you trouble. Gan Bik and a guard will go with you. It's the sensible thing to do."

He watched the man decide that it would be a good idea to be able to tell Siauw that the Machmurs were so sure the prisoners would be sent on that they provided an important escort—Gan Bik. "Okay."

Nick got Gan Bik aside. "Take a good man and fly up in Loponusias' plane and bring Muller and a Jap sailor down here. If there is any trouble come back quickly yourself."

"Trouble?"

"Buduk is in Judas' pay."

Nick watched Gan Bik's illusions shatter, crumbling in his eyes like a thin vase tapped with a metal bar. "Not Buduk."

"Yes, Buduk. You heard the story of the capture of Nife and Muller. And the fight."

"Of course. My father has been on the telephone all day. The families are confused, but some have agreed to action. Resistance."

"And Adam?"

"He will resist—I think."

"And your father?"

"He says fight. He is urging Adam to discard the idea that you can use bribes to solve everything." Gan Bik spoke with pride.

Nick said gently, "Your father is a smart man. Does he trust Buduk?"

"No. I did, because when we were young Buduk talked to us a lot. But if he was in Judas' pay—it explains a lot of things. I mean—he excused some things he did, but—"

"Like raising hell with women when he got to Djakarta?"

"How did you know that?"

"You know how news travels in Indonesia."

Adam and Ong Tjang drove Nick and Hans to the house. He was stretched out on a chaise lounge in the giant living room, his weight raised off his sore buttock, when he heard the growling rumble of the flying boat taking off. Nick looked at Ong. "Your son is a good man. I hope he gets the prisoners without trouble."

"If it can be done, he will do it." Ong hid his pride.

Tala came into the room as Nick changed his glance to Adam. Both she and her father started as he asked, "And where is your brave son, Akim?"

Adam regained his poker face at once. Tala looked at her hands. "Yes, Akim," Nick said. "Tala's twin brother who looks so much like her the deception was easy. She fooled us in Hawaii for awhile. Even one of Akim's teachers thought she was her brother when he took a quick look and studied photos."

Adam said to his daughter, "Tell him. The need for deception is about done anyway. By the time Judas finds out we'll be fighting him or we'll be dead."

Tala lifted her beautiful eyes to Nick, pleading for understanding. "It was Akim's idea. I was terrified when they had me prisoner. You can see—things—in Judas' eyes. When Muller brought me in in the launch to be seen and to have daddy make a payment, our people pretended their boat wouldn't run. Muller came in to the dock."

She faltered. Nick said, "Sounds like a brave operation. And Muller is a bigger fool than I thought. Senile. Go on."

"Everybody was friendly. Daddy presented him with some bottles and they had a drink. Akim had a skirt rolled up and a—a stuffed bra—and he talked to me and hugged me and when we parted—he pushed me off into the crowd and slumped down in their launch. They thought it was me crouched over crying. I wanted the families to rescue all the prisoners but they wanted to wait and pay. So I went to Hawaii and talked to you—"

"And you learned to be a first-class sub sailor," Nick said. "You kept the switch quiet because you hoped to keep Judas fooled and if it was known in Djakarta, you knew he'd find out about it in hours?"

"Yes," Adam said.

"You might have told me the truth," Nick said with a sigh. "It would have speeded things up a little."

"We didn't know you at first," Adam protested.

"I think things have speeded up a lot as it is." Nick saw the mischievous twinkle return to her eyes.

Ong Tjang coughed. "What is our next move, Mr. Bard?"

"Wait."

"Wait? How long. For what?"

"I don't know how long, or really for what, until our opponent moves. It is like a game of chess when you are in a superior position but your checkmate will depend on the move he chooses. He can't win, but he can do damage or delay the outcome. You shouldn't object to waiting. That used to be your policy."

Adam and Ong exchanged looks. This *Orang American* would make an excellent trader. Nick hid a grin. He wished he was really sure that Judas had no move to avoid checkmate.

Nick found the waiting easy. He slept long hours, bathed his wounds gently and began to go swimming when the cuts closed, walked about the colorful, exotic countryside, and learned to like *gado-gado*—a delicious blend of mixed vegetables with peanut sauce.

Gan Bik returned with Muller and the sailor and the prisoners were locked in the Machmur's sturdy jail. After a brief visit to note that the bars were strong and that two guards were always on duty, Nick ignored them. He borrowed Adam's new twenty-eight-foot runabout and took Tala for a picnic and island sightseeing trip. She seemed to think that by revealing the trick she and her brother had played, her bond with "Al Bard" was cemented. She virtually raped him as they rocked in a quiet lagoon, but he told himself he was too badly wounded to resist—it might open one of the cuts. When she asked him why he was chuckling he said, "Wouldn't it be funny if my blood got smeared on your legs and Adam saw it and jumped to conclusions and shot me?"

She didn't think it was funny at all.

He knew Gan Bik was suspicious of the depth of the relationship between Tala and the big American, but it was plain that the Chinese lad deluded himself that Nick was just a "big brother." Gan Bik brought his problems to Nick, most of them concerned with trying to modernize economic, labor and social practices on Fong Island. Nick pleaded lack of experience. "Get experts. I'm not your man."

But in one area he did offer advice. Gan Bik, as a captain in Adam Machmur's private army, was trying to raise the morale of his men and indoctrinate them with reasons for loyalty to Fong Island. He told Nick, "Our troops have always been for sale. You could damn near hold up a bundle of banknotes on a battlefield and buy 'em right there."

"Does that prove they're dumb or very smart?" Nick mused.

"You joke," Gan Bik exclaimed. "Troops must be loyal. To country. To commander."

"But these are private troops. Militia. I saw the regular army. Guarding big shots' homes and shaking down storekeepers."

"Yes. That is sad. We do not have the efficiency of German troops or the Gung Ho of Americans or the dedication of Japanese—"

"Thank God—"

"What?"

"Nothing much." Nick sighed. "Look—I think in the case of militia you have to give them two things to fight for. The first is self-interest. So promise them bonuses for action and top marksmanship. Then develop team spirit. Give prizes, medals and flags for the best units."

"Yes," Gan Bik said thoughtfully, "you have good suggestions. Men will show more enthusiasm for things they can see and feel personally. Like fighting for their land. *Then* you have no morale problem."

The next morning Nick noticed the troops drilling with extra enthusiasm, swinging their arms real wide-sweep Aussie style. Gan Bik had promised them something. Later that day Hans brought him a long cablegram as he lounged on the veranda, a pitcher of fruit punch beside him, enjoying a book he had found in Adam's bookcase.

Hans said, "The cable office phoned it so I know what's in it. Bill Rohde is in a sweat. What did you send him? What kind of tops?"

Hans had copied in block letters the cablese of Bill Rohde, the AXE agent fronting as manager for the "Bard Galleries." The sheet read: MOBBED FOR TOPS STOP TIMES AD REACHED EVERY WOULDBE HIPPIE STOP SHIP TWELVE GROSS.

Nick threw back his head and roared. Hans said, "Let me in on it."

"I shipped Bill a lot of yo-yo tops with religious carvings and nice scenes on them. Had to give Josef Dalam some business. Bill must have put an ad in the Times and sold all the damn things. Twelve gross! If he's selling them at the price I suggested we'll make—about four thousand bucks! And if the silly things keep on selling—"

"If you get home soon enough you can demonstrate them on TV," Hans said. "In a male Bikini. All the gals will—"

"Have some punch." Nick rattled the ice in the pitcher. "Please ask that girl to bring in the extension phone. I want to call Josef Dalam."

Hans rattled off some Indonesian. "You're getting lazy and indolent like all the rest of us."

"It's a good way of life."

"So you admit it?"

"Sure." The cute, well-built maid handed him the telephone with a big smile and a slow recovery of her hand as Nick ran his large fingers over her tiny ones. He watched her revolve away as if he could see through the sarong. "It's a wonderful country."

But without good telephone service. It took him half an hour to reach Dalam and tell him to ship the yo-yos.

That evening Adam Machmur put on the feast-and-dance he had promised. The guests watched colorful spectacles as groups performed and played and sang. Hans whispered to Nick, "This country is vaudeville twenty-four hours a day. When it stops here it still goes on in government offices."

"But they're happy. Having fun. Look at Tala dancing with all those girls. Rockettes with curves—"

"Sure. But as long as they breed the way they do, the genetic intelligence level will drop. In the end—the slums of India, like the worst ones you saw along the river in Djakarta."

"Hans, you're a gloom carrier."

"And we Hollanders cured disease right and left and discovered vitamins and improved sanitation."

Nick put a freshly opened bottle of beer into his friend's hand.

They played tennis the next morning. Although Nick won, he found Hans to be good competition. As they walked back to the house Nick said, "I absorbed what you said last night about over-breeding. Any way out?"

"In my opinion, none. They're doomed, Nick. They'll multiply like fruitflies on an apple until they're standing on each other's shoulders."

"I hope you're wrong. I hope something is discovered before it's too late."

"Like what? The answers are in man's reach but the generals and the politicians and the medicine men are blocking them. You know they always look backward. We'll see the day when—"

Nick never found out what they would see. Gan Bik ran around the corner of a thick spiked hedge. He gasped out, "Colonel Sudirmat is at the house demanding Muller and the sailor."

"That's interesting," Nick said. "Relax. Get your breath."

"But come *on*. Adam may let him have them."

Nick said, "Hans—please go up to the house. Get Adam or Ong aside and ask them just to stall Sudirmat for two hours. Get him to take a swim—have lunch—anything."

"Right." Hans walked swiftly away.

Gan Bik was shifting his weight from foot to foot, eager and excited.

"Gan Bik, how many men did Sudirmat bring with him?"

"Three."

"Where is the rest of his force?"

"How did you know he has a force nearby?"

"Guesswork."

"It's a good guess. They are at Gimbo, about fifteen miles down the second valley. Sixteen trucks and about a hundred men and two heavy machine guns and an old one-pounder."

"Nice going. Your scouts are watching them?"

"Yes."

"What about attacks from other directions? Sudirmat is no dope."

"He has two companies on stand-by at Bintho barracks. They can hit us from any of several directions, but we'll know when they leave Bintho and we'll probably know which way they are coming."

"What have you got for heavy firepower?"

"A forty-millimeter and three Swedish machine guns. Plento of ammo and explosives for making mines."

"Your boys have been practicing making mines?"

Gan Bik struck a fist against a palm. "They enjoy it. Pow!"

"Have them mine the road from Gimbo at a road block that cannot be taken easily. Hold the rest of your boys in reserve until we hear which way the Bintho detachment may come in."

"You're sure they'll attack?"

"Sooner or later they'll have to, if they want their little stuffed shirt back."

Gan Bik chuckled and trotted off. Nick found Hans with Adam and Ong Tjang and Colonel Sudirmat on the broad veranda. Hans said pointedly, "Nick, you remember the Colonel. Better wash up, old man, we're about to go in to lunch."

At the big table used by senior guests and Adam's own groups there was a feeling of expectancy. It was broken when Sudirmat said, "Mr. Bard—I came to ask Adam for the two men you brought here from Sumatra."

"Did you?"

Sudirmat looked puzzled, as if he had been tossed a rock instead of a ball. "Did I—what?"

"Did you really? And what did Mr. Machmur say?"

"He said he must speak to you at luncheon—and here we are."

"The men are international criminals. I really should turn them in to Djakarta."

"Oh no, I am the authority here. You should not have moved them out of Sumatra, much less into my area. You are in serious trouble, Mr. Bard. It will cost you a lot of time and expense before this mess is settled. You—"

"Colonel, you have said enough. I am not releasing the prisoners."

"Mr. Bard—you are still wearing that pistol." Sudirmat shook his head sadly from side to side. He was shifting the subject, searching for a way to put his man on the defensive. He wanted to dominate the situation—he had heard all about how this Al Bard had fought and killed a man with two knives. And one of Judas' men, at that!

"Yes, I am." Nick gave him a wide smile. "It gives one a feeling of security and confidence when facing untrustworthy, treacherous, selfish, greedy, perfidious, dishonest colonels." He drawled the words, allowing plenty of time in case their English was slow with the exact meanings.

Sudirmat flushed, straightened in his seat. He was not a complete coward, although most of his personal scores were settled by a sucker shot in the back or a hireling's "Texas Court"—a shotgun from ambush. "Your words are insulting."

"Not as much as they are factual. You've been working for Judas and double-crossing your own countrymen ever since Judas started his operation."

Gan Bik entered the room, spotted Nick, and came to him with a note open in his hand. "This just came in."

Nick nodded to Sudirmat as politely as if they had interrupted a discussion of cricket scores. He read: *All departing Gimbo 1250 hours. Preparing leave Bintho.*

Nick smiled up at the lad. "Excellent. Carry on." He let Gan Bik reach the doorway, then called, "Oh, Gan—" Nick got up and hurried after the youth, who stopped and turned. Nick murmured, "Capture his three soldiers that are here."

"Men are watching them now. Just waiting my order."

"You don't have to reach me about blocking the Bintho force. When you know their route—block them."

Gan Bik showed his first sign of worry. "They can bring up a lot more troops. Artillery. How long must we hold them?"

"Just a few hours—perhaps till tomorrow morning." Nick laughed and patted his shoulder. "You trust me, don't you?"

"Of course." Gan Bik trotted off and Nick shook his head. First too suspicious—now too trusting. He went back to the table.

Colonel Sudirmat was saying to Adam and Ong, "My troops will be here shortly. Then we will see who calls names—"

Nick said: "Your troops have moved out as ordered. And they have been stopped cold. Now speaking of pistols —hand over that popgun on your belt. Hold it with your fingers on the handle."

Sudirmat's favorite diversion, next to rape, was watching American movies. Westerns were shown every night when he was at his command post. Old ones with Tom Mix and Hoot Gibson—new ones with John Wayne and modern stars who had to be helped onto their horses. But the Indonesians did not know that. Many of them thought that *all* Americans are cowboys. Sudirmat had practiced his fast draw faithfully—but these Americans were born with guns on them! He carefully passed his Czechoslovakian automatic across the table, holding it lightly between his fingers.

Adam said worriedly, "Mr. Bard—are you sure—"

"Mr. Machmur, you will be too in a very few minutes. Let's lock this turd up and I'll show you."

Ong Tjang said, "Turd? I don't know that. In French— German please—it means—?"

Nick said, "Horse apples." Sudirmat scowled as Nick pointed the way to the guard house.

Gan Bik and Tala stopped Nick as he left the jail. Gan Bik carried a combat radio. He looked worried. "Eight more trucks are coming to back up the ones from Bintho."

"Have you got a strong roadblock?"

"Yes. Or if we blow Tapaci bridge—"

"Blow it. Does your amphib pilot know where it is?"

"Yes."

"How much dynamite can you spare me here—now?"

"A lot. Forty—fifty sticks."

"Get it for me at the plane and then go back up your men. Hold that road. Blow the bridge."

As Gan Bik nodded Tala asked, "What can I do?"

Nick studied the two youngsters. "Stay with Gan. Collect first aid equipment and if you've got some courageous girls like yourself take them along. There may be casualties."

The amphibian pilot knew Tapaci bridge. He pointed it out with the same enthusiasm with which he had watched Nick tape the soft sticks of explosive together, bind them with wire for added security and insert a cap—two inches of metal like a miniature ballpoint pen—deep in each group with a yard-long fuse trailing from it. He taped the fuse to the package so that it would not jolt off. "Boom!" the pilot said delightedly. "Boom. There."

The narrow Tapaci bridge was a smoking ruin. Gan Bik had radioed his demolition team and they knew their business. Nick yelled into the flyer's ear. "Make a nice easy pass straight down the road. Let's scatter 'em and blow a truck or two if we can."

They unloaded the sputtering homemade bombs in two passes. If Sudirmat's men knew anti-aircraft drill, they forgot it or never thought of it. When last seen they were running in all directions from the column of trucks, three of which were burning.

"Home," Nick told the pilot.

They never made it. The engine quit ten minutes later and they landed in a quiet lagoon. The pilot grinned cheerfully. "I know. Gas line. Lousy gas. I'll fix."

Nick sweated right along with him. Using a set of tools that looked like a Woolworth's home repair kit they stripped and cleaned the lines.

Nick sweated and fretted because they had lost three hours. Finally, with raw gas priming her carburetors the engine caught on the first spin and they were flying again. "Look offshore near Fong," Nick shouted, "a sailing vessel ought to be there."

It was. The *Oporto* lay to near Machmur's docks. Nick said, "Go across Zoo Island. You may know it as Adata—next to Fong."

The engine quit once more over Zoo's solid carpet of green. Nick shuddered. What a way to go, speared by trees in a jungle crack-up. The young pilot stretched the glide down the creek valley up which Nick had climbed with Tala and put the old amphibian down outside the surf line like a leaf falling on a pond. Nick took a deep breath. He received a big grin from the pilot. "We clean the lines again."

"You do it. I'll be back in a couple of hours."

"Okay."

Nick trotted along the beach. Wind and water had already changed landmarks but this had to be the place. He was the right distance from the creek mouth. He studied the headlands and trotted on. All the banyans at the jungle's edge looked alike. Where were the hawsers?

A menacing crash in the jungle caused him to crouch and draw Wilhelmina. Bursting through the underbrush, sweeping aside two-inch limbs like toothpicks, came Mabel! The ape skipped across the sand, put her head against Nick's shoulder and her arm around him and signed happily. He lowered the gun. "Hello, baby. They'll never believe this back home."

She made happy, cooing sounds.

Chapter 8

NICK walked on, digging in the sand on the seaward side of the banyan trees. Nothing. The ape followed at his shoulder like a champion dog or a faithful wife. She watched him, then skipped ahead along the beach; stopped and looked back as if to say, "Come on."

"No," Nick said. "This is all impossible. But if this is your hunk of beach—"

It was. Mabel stopped at the seventh tree and scooped up two lines from under the sand which the tides had brought in. Nick patted her shoulder.

Twenty minutes later he had the little sub's flotation tanks pumped out and the engine warmed. His last glimpse of the small bay was of Mabel standing on the shore raising one great arm questioningly. He thought her expression was heartbroken, but he told himself it was his imagination.

He soon surfaced hear the amphibian and told the bug-eyed pilot he would meet him at the Machmurs'. "I won't reach there till dark. If you want to fly over the roadblocks to find out if the army is planning any tricks, go ahead. Can you reach Gan Bik by radio?"

"No. I drop him a note."

The young airman dropped no notes that afternoon. As he brought the slow amphibian in toward the ramp, settling toward the sea like a fat beetle, he passed very near the *Oporto*. She was clearing for action and switching her identity to that of a junk. Judas had heard the army's intercoms yelling at the Tapaci bridge. Judas' anti-aircraft quick-firers cut the plane to ribbons and it plopped into the water like a tired bug. The pilot had not been hit. He shrugged and swam ashore.

It was dark when Nick slipped the sub up to Machmur's fuel dock and topped off its tanks. The four lads on the docks spoke little English but they kept repeating, "Go house. See Adam. Quick."

He found Hans, Adam, Ong and Tala on the porch. A dozen men guarded the position—it looked like a command post. Hans said, "Welcome back. There's hell to pay."

"What happened?"

"Judas sneaked ashore and raided the guardhouse. He freed Muller and the Jap and Sudirmat. There was a crazy struggle for the guards' arms—there were only two men left on guard there as Gan Bik took all the troops with him. Then Sudirmat was shot by one of his own men and the others went off with Judas."

"The perils of despotism. I wonder how long that soldier was waiting for his chance. Is Gan Bik holding the roads?"

"Like a rock. Our worry is Judas. He can shell us or make another foray. He sent a message to Adam. He wants $150,000. In one week."

"Or he kills Akim?"

"Yes."

Tala started to cry. Nick said, "Don't, Tala. Don't worry, Adam, I'll get the prisoners back." If he was over-confident, he thought, it was in a good cause.

He drew Hans aside, scribbled a message on a pad. "Are the telephones still working?"

"Sure Sudirmat's adjutant calls every ten minutes with threats."

"Try and phone this to the cable office."

The cable Hans repeated carefully into the phone read: ADVISE CHINA BANK JUDAS COLLECTED SIX MILLION GOLD AND NOW LINKED TO NAHDATUL ULAMA PARTY. It was dispatched to David Hawk.

Nick addressed Adam, "Send a man with guts out to Judas. Tell him you'll pay him the $150,000 at ten A.M. tomorrow if you can have Akim back at once."

"I don't have that much money here in hard currency. I won't take Akim if the other prisoners must die. No Machmur could ever show his face again—"

"We aren't paying them anything and we're getting all the prisoners free. It's a trick."

"Oh." He issued rapid orders.

At dawn Nick was in the little sub, rocking in the shallows at periscope depth a half-mile down the beach from the trim Chinese junk *Butterfly Wind* flying Chiang Kai-shek's flag, a red duster with a white sun in blue dexter canton. Nick had the sub's antenna up. He scanned the frequencies endlessly. He heard chatter from the army's radios at the roadblocks, he heard Gan Bik's firm tones and knew that everything was probably all right out there. Then he got the strong signal—nearby—and the *Butterfly Wind's* radio answered.

Nick set his transmitter on the same frequency and repeated endlessly, "Hello *Butterfly Wind*. Hello Judas. We have the communist prisoners for you and the money. Hello *Butterfly Wind*—"

He kept talking as he sailed the little submerged craft toward the junk, not sure if the sea would damp-out his signal but theoretically the periscope-rigged antenna would transmit at this depth.

Judas swore and stamped on the floor of his cabin and switched to his high-powered transmitter. It did not have the intercom crystals and he could not raise the unseen vessel which was standing a CW code watch on the high-power bands. "Muller," he grated, "what is this devil trying to do? Listen."

Muller said, "It's close. If the corvette believes *that,* we're in trouble, Try the DF—"

"Bah. I don't need the DF. It's that madman Bard from shore. Can you rig the transmitter for enough power to blot him?"

"It will take a little time."

Nick watched the *Butterfly Wind* enlarge in the viewing glass. He swept the sea with the scope and saw a vessel on the horizon. He took the small sub down six feet, peeping with the metal eye at intervals as he approached the junk from the shoreward side. The eyes of her lookouts should be on the ship coming in from the sea. He reached the starboard bow without being discovered. When he opened the hatch he heard the masthead lookout yelling with a bullhorn, other men shouting, and the boom of a heavy gun. A spout of water erupted fifty yards from the junk.

"That'll keep you busy," Nick muttered as he tossed a nylon covered grappling iron up to catch on a scupper's metal rim. "Wait'll they correct the range." He went swiftly up the line and peeked over the deck's edge.

Boom! A shell *whirrrrred* past the mainmast, its ugly purr so strong you imagined you could feel a gust from its passage. Everybody on board clustered at the seaward side, yelling, roaring with bullhorns. Muller directed two men signaling semaphore and international Morse flags. Nick chuckled—nothing you can tell them now will make them happy! He climbed aboard and vanished down the forward hatch. He catfooted along a companionway, down another ladder—from Gan Bik's and Tala's descriptions and drawings he felt as if he had been here before.

The prisoners' guard reached for his sidearm and Wilhelmina barked. Through the throat at exact center. Nick unlocked the cell. "C'mon, lads."

"There's one more," a tough-looking youngster said. "Give me the keys."

The youth released Akim. Nick gave the guard's gun to the lad who had demanded the keys and watched him check the safety. He would do.

On deck Muller froze as he saw Nick and the seven young Indonesians pop out of the hatchway and leap overside. The old Nazi ran to the poop for his Tommy gun, sprayed the sea with slugs. He might as well have shot at a school of porpoises hiding underwater.

A three-inch shell hit the junk amidships, exploded inboard, and blasted Muller to his knees. He limped painfully aft to confer with Judas.

Nick surfaced at the sub, wrenched open the hatch, vaulted into the tiny cockpit and got the tiny vessel underway without a waste motion. The boys clung to it like waterbugs on a turtle's back. Nick yelled, "Watch for shots! Go overboard if you see guns!"

"Ja."

The opposition was busy. Muller yelled to Judas, "The prisoners got away! How can we stop those fools shooting? They've gone crazy!"

Judas was cool as a merchant captain watching boat drill. He had known the day of reckoning with the dragon would come—but so soon! At such a poor time! He said, "Put your Nelson's suit on now, Muller. You will know just how he felt."

He trained his binoculars on the corvette and his lip curled grimly as he saw the colors of the People's Republic of China. He lowered the glasses and cackled—a weird, guttural sound like a demon's curse. "Ja, Muller— you can sound abandon ship. Our deal with the Chicoms is being dissolved."

Two rounds from the corvette blew a hole in the junk's bow and blasted her 40mm. gun into scrap. Nick made a mental note as he headed for shore at full power—except for their ranging shots those gunners never missed.

Hans met him at the dock. "Looks like Hawk got the cable and spread the word just right."

Adam Machmur ran up and embraced his son.

The junk burned, settling slowly. The corvette grew smaller on the horizon. "How will you bet, Hans?" Nick asked. "Is that Judas' finish or not?"

"No bet. From what we know about him he could be escaping in a scuba outfit right now."

"Let's take a boat and see what we can find."

They found part of the crew clinging to wreckage, four bodies, two badly wounded. Of Judas and Muller there was no sign. As they gave up the search at nightfall Hans commented, "I hope they're in sharks' bellies."

At the conference the next morning Adam Machmur was his composed, calculating self again. "The families are grateful. It was masterfully done, Mr. Bard. Planes will be here soon to pick up the boys."

"What about the army and explaining Sudirmat's death?" Nick asked.

Adam smiled. "With our combined influence and testimony—the army will be reprimanded. It can all be blamed on Colonel Sudirmat's greed."

The private amphibian of the Wan King clan delivered Nick and Hans to Djakarta. At dusk Nick—showered and in fresh clothes—awaited Mata in the cool, shadowy living room in which he had enjoyed so may perfumed hours. She arrived and came straight to his arms. "You're really safe! I heard the most fantastic stories. They're all over the city."

"Some may be true, my sweet. Most important— Sudirmat is dead. The hostages are freed. Judas' pirate ship is destroyed."

She kissed him hotly. "—all over."

"Almost."

"Almost? Come—I'll change and you tell me about it—"

He explained very little as he watched with admiring

fascination as she tossed her city clothes aside and wrapped herself in a flowered sarong.

When they went to the patio and settled down with gin and tonics she asked, "What will you do now?"

"I must leave. And I want you to come with me."

Her beautiful face was radiant as she stared at him with surprise and delight. "What? Ah, yes—Do you really—"

"*Really*, Mata. You must come with me. Within forty-eight hours. I'll leave you at Singapore or anywhere you wish. And you must never return to Indonesia." He looked into her eyes, grave and intent. "You must *never* return to Indonesia. If you do, then I must return and—make some changes."

She paled. There was something deep and unreadable in his gray eyes which were as hard as burnished steel. She understood, but she tried once more. "But if I decide I don't want to? I mean—with you is one thing—but to be cast aside in Singapore—"

"You're too dangerous to leave behind, Mata. If I do that I won't have completed my job—and I'm always thorough. You operate for money, not ideology, so I can make you the offer. If you stay?" He sighed. "You had many contacts other than Sudirmat. Your pipelines and the web by which you communicated with Judas are still intact. I imagine you used the military radio—or you may have your own people. But . . . you see . . . my position."

She felt chilled. This was not the man she had held in her arms, almost the first man in her life she had linked with thoughts of love. A man so strong, virile, tender, with a keen mind—but how steely those handsome eyes were now! "I didn't think you—"

He touched her lips and closed them with a finger. "You stepped into several traps. You will remember them. Corruption breeds carelessness. Seriously, Mata—I suggest you accept my first offer."

"And your second—?" Her throat was suddenly dry. She remembered the pistol and the knife he wore, putting them aside and out of sight with a quiet joke when she commented on them. From the corner of her eye she looked again at the implacable mask which looked so strange on the beloved, handsome face. Her hand rose to her mouth and she paled. "You would! Yes ... you killed Nife. And Judas and the others. You are ... different from Hans Nordenboss."

"I am different," he agreed with quiet seriousness. "If you ever set foot in Indonesia again, I will kill you."

He hated the words, but the deal must be explicitly pictured. No—fatal misunderstanding. She cried for hours, wilted like a flower in a drought, seeming to wring all her vitality out of herself with the tears. He regretted the scene—but he knew the power of recovery of beautiful females. Another country—other men—and probably other deals.

She repulsed him—then crept into his arms and in a tiny voice said, "I know I have no choice. I will go."

He relaxed—just a little. "I'll help you. Nordenboss can be trusted to sell what you leave behind and I guarantee you will get the money. You won't be in a new country penniless."

She choked off a final sob and her fingers caressed his chest. "Can you spare a day or two to help me get settled in Singapore?"

"I think so."

Her body seemed to be without bones. It was surrender. Nick gave a slow, soft sigh of relief. You never got used to it. This way was better. Hawk would approve.

Dear Reader:

We want to thank you for buying this AWARD paperback book, and we do hope that you enjoyed it.

Our aim is to publish books that you want to read. Therefore, we would like to ask a few questions concerning your personal reading habits and preferences.

If you will check off your answers to the questions listed below and return to Award Books, Dept. RJA, 235 E. 45th Street, New York, New York 10017, we will be happy to send you a complimentary copy of one of AWARD's current releases as our way of saying, "Thank you."

1. I decided to read this book because of:
   ____Personal recommendation
   ____Advertising. Where?   ____TV ____Radio ____Newspaper
                              ____Magazine
   ____Book cover
   ____Knew of hard cover edition
   ____Other

2. Where did you purchase this book?
   ____Book Store   ____Rail or Bus Terminal
   ____Newsstand   ____Discount Store
   ____Airport   ____Department Store
   ____Supermarket   ____Other

3. My favorite book categories are:
   ____Mysteries   ____Police-Action
   ____Westerns   ____Movie Tie-Ins
   ____Science Fiction   ____Health and Fitness
   ____Mystic and Occult   ____Cook Books
   ____Antiques   ____Diet

4. I read on the average (paperback):
   ____Under three books a year   ____6 to 12 books a year
   ____3 to 6 books a year   ____Over 12

5. My age is:
   ____Under 18   ____18 to 24
   ____25 to 34   ____35 to 49
   ____50 to 64   ____65 and over

6. My education (check highest):
   ____High School   ____College Graduate
   ____Attended College   ____Post-Graduate School

Name_____

Address_____

City_____State_____Zip_____

AQ1501

AWARD BOOKS

NICK CARTER

Don't Miss A Single High-Tension Novel In The Nick Carter Killmaster Series

COUNTERFEIT AGENT   Nick Carter
Killmaster faces a hydra-headed army of assassins that threatens to turn an international peace conference into a bloody massacre!
AQ1439—$1.25

TARGET: DOOMSDAY ISLAND   Nick Carter
A treacherous nuclear arsenal is concealed on a billionaire's island paradise. And the U.S. is targeted for invasion.
AQ1414—$1.25

THE JERUSALEM FILE   Nick Carter
The world's ten wealthiest men have been kidnapped. AXE's rescue plan pits Carter against murderous Arab terrorists.
AQ1400—$1.25

DEATH OF THE FALCON   Nick Carter
Arab fanatics launch a harrowing terror campaign that threatens to trigger a worldwide holocaust.
AQ1354—$1.25

THE N3 CONSPIRACY   Nick Carter
Africa—white slavers, rebel commandos, vicious mercenaries—and Killmaster fights for survival!
AQ1332—$1.25

THE MAN WHO SOLD DEATH   Nick Carter
"Blistering excitement!"—King Features. A plot to corner the gold market through murder, theft and international sabotage!
AQ1297—$1.25

THE HUMAN TIME BOMB   Nick Carter
Killmaster alone against an army of programmed assassins!
AQ1474—$1.25

USE HANDY, MONEY-SAVING ORDER FORM ON BACK PAGE

"NICK CARTER OUT-BONDS JAMES BOND!"
—BUFFALO NEWS

AGENT COUNTER-AGENT — Nick Carter
A bizarre threat to American sovereignty catapults Nick into a mind-bending game of wits and nerves with the notorious KGB.
AQ1477—$1.25

ASSASSINATION BRIGADE — Nick Carter
Killmaster faces an army of kamikaze slaves and a mad super-genius bent on world conquest!
AQ1456—$1.25

ASSASSIN: CODE NAME VULTURE — Nick Carter
Killmaster must stop the bloody coup-masters led by the international assassin named Vulture!
AQ1454—$1.25

MASSACRE IN MILAN — Nick Carter
Arab terrorists, Nazi spies and Israeli counter-agents—colliding in a deadly game of oil diplomacy and espionage.
AQ1455—$1.25

RUSH YOUR ORDER TODAY!

AWARD BOOKS,
350 Kennedy Drive, Hauppauge, N.Y. 11788

Please send me the books checked below by number:

☐ AQ1439	$1.25	☐ AQ1474	$1.25
☐ AQ1414	$1.25	☐ AQ1477	$1.25
☐ AQ1400	$1.25	☐ AQ1456	$1.25
☐ AQ1354	$1.25	☐ AQ1454	$1.25
☐ AQ1332	$1.25	☐ AQ1455	$1.25
☐ AQ1297	$1.25		

I am enclosing $_____

SAVE $ $ $ 5 books or more, deduct 10% discount
DISCOUNT   8 books or more, deduct 15% discount
PLAN   10 books or more, deduct 20% discount

Name_____

Address_____

City_____ State_____ Zip_____

Add 25¢ for postage and handling for one book, 35¢ for two or three books. We pay postage on all orders of four books or more. Send remittance in U.S. or Canadian funds. Sorry, no C.O.D.s.